Andrew Leigh

Conversations with Remarkable Women

ISBN 978-1-0369-0685-6

CONTENTS

NOTES

INTRODUCTION

How often have I read a biography and even an autobiography and wondered: "But what would it be like to sit opposite this person for real and be able to talk to them? I am not alone in such an ambition. For example, concluding his absorbing biography of the nineteenth-century surgeon and gynaecologist Samuel Pozzi, author Julian Barnes admits that his "time spent in the distant, decadent, hectic, violent, narcissistic Belle Epoque has left me cheerful."

Talking with long-deceased historical figures is not quite as bizarre as it sounds. For example, Albert Einstein visualised conversations with past science talents such as Isaac Newton and James Clerk Maxwell when developing his theories. Such imaginary dialogues allowed him to test his ideas against the wisdom of other geniuses, pushing beyond traditional boundaries of thought.

Likewise, the 16th-century French philosopher Michel de Montaigne often engaged in imaginary conversations with Socrates, Seneca, and Plutarch. He claimed these interchanges allowed one to "rub and polish our brain by contact with others." Henry Ford, who invented the mass production of cars, relied on the advice and ideas of deceased individuals, particularly through what he called his "Master Mind" group. Ford was a student of Napoleon Hill, who encouraged the idea of consulting the wisdom of others, living or dead. Ford used this practice to harness the collective wisdom of successful individuals and saw the practice as a way to gain insights and creative solutions beyond his understanding.

Well-known motivational speaker Napoleon Hill also gained confidence by conversing with great achievers in his imagination, contributing to his real-world success. He shared his experiences engaging with historical figures such as Abraham Lincoln and Thomas Edison. He described how he would mentally sit down with them to discuss challenges and gather insights. "These people helped me in ways that were psychological and tangible."

Have a useful chat with the greats - see Note 1 at the end of this book.

WHY WOMEN?

For definite reasons, I have chosen to have conversations with women. First, for anyone doubting that the female of the species has experienced a rotten deal through the ages, Philippa Gregory's masterpiece, Normal Women, charts nine hundred years of their struggle and ability to make history. Despite this, there are countless tales of women and their singular achievements in a world that often tries to tune them out. For instance, the International Encyclopaedia of Contemporary Women Composers lists over 6,000 entries. Can you name just three?

An obvious conclusion from Gregory's work is that women of achievement are not only normal, but, above all, just people. While tempted to call these Conversations with Remarkable People, I realised that what most interests me is how often male prejudices, conscious or otherwise, burden women. It's mainly men who have built societies limiting women to an excruciatingly limited number of roles and prevented them from realising their full potential.

My second reason for wanting to converse with remarkable women springs from curiosity. I wanted to discover what meeting some of history's most compelling people would be like. Of course, most have been interviewed before, or their stories told vividly and in detail by historians and biographers. Yet, talking directly with them would still be fascinating and help me better understand their lives.

Third, conversations only with deceased women mainly arose from wanting to limit my choices and avoid trying to access some of the world's busiest people. People like pop icon Taylor Swift, Mary Barra, CEO of General Motors, Michelle Obama, and Rachel Reeves, Britain's first woman chancellor, understandably guard their time jealously.

WHAT LESSONS?

Author Frances Wilson calls her biography of D.H. Lawrence a work of non-fiction. Similarly, my conversations with remarkable women stem partly from my imagination. As George R.R. Martin, author of epic fantasy novels adapted into an Emmy Award-winning television series, comments, "Why risk reality when the imagination can be equally if not more compelling?"

Imagination helped literary genius Colette create unreal conversations between her cat and dog, requiring the reader to suspend any judgment about the reliability of such dialogues. To enjoy a feature film, a play, or a novel, you tacitly agree to put aside your assumptions about the nature of reality. You're asked to do the same with the twenty conversations in this book. You can trust that the ones here are firmly rooted in documented research and published material. Even so, I have felt free to ask questions and imagine my subjects' reactions and possible answers. If this approach leaves you wanting to be on more solid ground, check out the biographies that partly helped create them, which are listed at the end of each conversation.

WHO SHOULD I MEET?

Ultimately, I asked: Would I like to meet this person? Unless I could honestly say "Yes", they did not reach the shortlist. And what did I mean by 'remarkable'? All those I considered meeting were outstanding in every sense of the word. But I realised it was insufficient to say or do exceptional things. I wanted to meet those who had achieved a significant impact on the world despite the odds. Above all, I wished to meet them because of who they were as human beings.

Mentally, I thank all twenty women for my further education in understanding, at a deeper level than before, what each of these extraordinary yet ordinary people needed to do to succeed. So, which women should be selected out of the many possibilities? There seem seven main ways to select someone for a conversation:

- Historical Impact

- Cultural or Artistic Influence

- Pioneering Spirit

- Social Change & Activism

- Mythology and Legend

- Global Recognition

- Inspirational and enduring legacy

Remembering remarkable women - see Note 2 at the end of this book.

The final selection proved a tough ask. Madam Curie, whom I left out, almost insisted on being interviewed despite the many French female achievers already included. Others, like Elizabeth I of England, seemed strangely inaccessible. Some, like Florence Nightingale, had so much written about her that I preferred to meet her contemporary, the modest pioneer nurse and carer Mary Seacole.

Lastly, space has prevented me from including people from every country and walk of life equally. For instance, I included Catherine the Great of Russia but not China's incredible Empress Cixi.

So here are my twenty conversations with remarkable women. I am drawn to each person in some way, trusting they would probably make themselves available for a brief, imaginary moment if they could.

CATHERINE THE GREAT OF RUSSIA

1729–1796

Catherine the Great, Empress of Russia, expanded and modernised the Russian Empire during her reign. A powerful and enlightened monarch, she promoted Western ideals, wrote regularly to thinkers such as Voltaire, advanced education, and increased Russian influence in Europe. Known for her strong rule, cultural patronage, and sweeping reforms, she impacted Russia's political and cultural landscape.

"Power without a nation's confidence is nothing."

Memoirs of the Empress Catherine II, 1859

CATHERINE THE GREAT OF RUSSIA

It's 1794, and I am at the Winter Palace in St. Petersburg, eagerly awaiting a conversation with the Empress, now known to history as Catherine the Great. The prospect of meeting this extraordinary woman, who has steered Russia for over thirty years and continues to wield significant influence in European politics and culture, fills me with excitement and some apprehension.

The sheer grandeur of the Winter Palace overwhelms my senses. Countless frescoes enhance titanic ceilings, each embellished with intricate gilded mouldings. Enormous chandeliers make me think of the night sky glittering with stars. Unmissable, above the elaborate marble fireplace, is a heavily framed, colourful portrait of Catherine, resplendent in her imperial regalia.

Without warning, the Empress appears immobile in the doorway, regal and commanding. All that's missing from this gripping tableau is a sudden blast of trumpets. Despite her dignified, erect posture and magnificent surroundings, Catherine exudes a natural warmth that immediately puts me at ease. As I respectfully stand, she takes her time settling in a chair and then gestures that I should sit, too. From nowhere apparent, an interpreter discreetly emerges behind the Empress.

"Welcome to my Winter Palace," she says in slightly Russian-accentuated English.

Your Imperial Majesty, you are most generous in granting this audience for our Conversation. To begin, please let us speak a little about your origins. How on earth did a young girl from Prussia become the ruler of Russia?

"I appreciate the courtesy, but there's no need to address me as Your Imperial Majesty. Empress Catherine is sufficient. Secondly, it's my pleasure to have this opportunity to talk with someone who is so well-travelled. I was born in 1729 as Sophie Friederike Auguste von Anhalt-Zerbst in Prussia. My upbringing was typical for a German princess. My father was a minor prince, and while we weren't wealthy, we were undoubtedly of noble standing. Johanna, my mother, was a very ambitious woman with grand plans for me. She orchestrated my betrothal to the heir of the Russian throne, Grand Duke Peter, who would later become Emperor Peter III. Consequently, at 15, I was sent to Russia to meet him and to be groomed for my future role. To meet the imperial requirements of my new country and destiny, I converted to Orthodoxy, changing my name to Catherine—Yekaterina Alekseyevna."

Moving from a tiny German principality to the Russian court can't have been easy. How did you cope?

"Yes, it was extremely testing. So much was alien, yet I was determined to succeed. With a devotion bordering on passion, I mastered Russian history, the language, and my new Orthodox faith. I also made it my business to stay close to the powerful Imperial Guard. One year after arriving, I married Peter, though it was not a happy union. Despite that, I accepted that my future, and Russia's, would depend on my ability to navigate these challenges."

How did you become Empress on your own, without Peter? It seems such an unlikely event.

"You're right. Women in Russia are seldom considered politically aware or even capable of playing a role. Indeed, becoming Empress was not something I could ever have predicted. Peter was more interested in playing with his toy soldiers and imitating the Prussian court than ruling a vast empire like Russia. On the other hand, I found my calling in the political and cultural life of the court.

It happened like this: When Peter ascended the throne as Peter III, he immediately upset many of the Russian nobility and military by making hasty decisions, such as withdrawing from the Seven Years' War and forming an alliance with Frederick II of Prussia — an enemy of Russia at the time. You can be sure that it didn't take long for a conspiracy to form against him.

Whose idea was this conspiracy? Despite my research, I am unclear exactly how it occurred.

"No matter what you may have heard, the conspiracy wasn't entirely my doing, though I was aware of it and offered support."

Pausing for the interpreter to clarify her words, this most astute woman carefully studies my reactions. I realise with a slight shock that in answering, the Empress is not just speaking to me. She assumes a far wider audience: "The coup happened in July 1762, only six months after Peter became emperor. The Imperial Guard, loyal to me, arrested Peter, who quickly surrendered and was imprisoned. I was proclaimed Empress.

Tragically, Peter died later under mysterious circumstances. Please be clear: I did not order his death, though understandably, people often blame me for it. That is the nature of power, which too frequently comes at a heavy price."

Such a transition from Grand Duchess to Empress could not have been easy.

"I agree, but remember, I'd spent years educating myself, understanding the complexities of Russian politics, and aligning myself with powerful factions within the court, such as the Imperial Guard. From my involvement with all the power brokers, I won support to modernise Russia and bring it closer to the ideals of the European Enlightenment I admired."

Since you mentioned the Enlightenment, you have had a lengthy correspondence with Voltaire, the Enlightenment thinker. He takes a famously dim view of autocracy and often criticises it in his writing.

"That's true. We had an extraordinary correspondence starting in the early 1760s. I valued Voltaire's insights and often sought his advice on matters of state and reform. I admired him, though there was always tension since he favoured liberty and reform, and I was what he called an autocratic ruler. In our letters, we discussed philosophy, literature, governance, and my reforms in Russia. Voltaire admired my efforts to modernise Russia, seeing me as a ruler who could bring Enlightenment ideals to my country. I was bereft when he died in 1778 since I relished his perspectives to help shape my policies and reforms.

Even so, Empress, he was critical of your absolute power, right?

"I agree. But he saw me as an exception. He thought an enlightened absolute ruler should use power to adopt rational and progressive policies. We both agreed that in making reforms to a vast and relatively undeveloped country like Russia, an enlightened autocracy might be more effective than a democratic system. We concluded that governing well in these circumstances requires a firm hand."

Can you explain more on this?

"While I believed in the Enlightenment, I also judged that to keep Russia united and secure, it was essential to maintain a strong, centralised power. Sometimes, I had to put down revolts, such as the Pugachev's Rebellion and his claim to be my late husband, Peter III. This pretender incited a massive peasant uprising, and I had to use force to crush it. It was a brutal and bloody affair lasting two years. Such are the contradictions of my rule. A deep commitment to progress and Enlightenment tempered by the harsh realities of governing an empire as vast and diverse as Russia."

One of your significant reforms is the new legal code, most of which you wrote yourself.

"Not most, all of it! The Nakaz, or Instruction, was a labour of love inspired by Montesquieu's 'The Spirit of the Laws' and Beccaria's ideas on criminal justice. I aimed to reform Russia's legal system to promote equality before the law and eliminate the use of torture. Sadly, there was strong resistance from the nobility, eager to avoid having their privileges curtailed. The Nakaz has never been fully implemented, but it's a start. It attempts to steer Russia toward a more just and rational society."

Apart from reforming the legal system, what do you regard as critical moments of your reign?

"Ah, there are many such moments, both triumphant and challenging. Beyond the Pugachev Rebellion, which tested my resolve, several key events have affected my rule and Russia's future. One of the most significant is the expansion of the Russian Empire. Russia's borders have grown considerably under my reign.

And domestically, Empress, what do you see as critical moments?

"As I am sure you know, I have also made great efforts to modernise Russia's economy and government. The Free Economic Society, which I established, encourages agricultural innovation. We have invited European experts to Russia to help improve our industries. I have also reorganised provincial governments, granting local authorities more freedom while ensuring they remain loyal to the crown.

One of my triumphs is supporting the arts, transforming the Russian court into a centre of European culture. For example, my private art collection, The Hermitage, began as a modest gallery but has become one of the world's largest and most renowned collections. I'm an avid collector of art, literature, and scientific instruments. Apart from my connection to Voltaire, I continue to correspond with other great minds of our time.

Of course, not everything has gone as I've hoped. My attempts at serf reform, for example, have mainly failed. Although I wanted to improve the lives of the serfs, the nobility fear losing power and influence. So, the peasant class remains oppressed, and this remains one of my lasting regrets. It will have to change one day, but I probably won't live to see it."

One aspect of your reign you surely do not regret is your relationship with Grigory Potemkin. Can you speak about that, please?

"You touch on such a sensitive matter for me to discuss. Grigory Potemkin was a remarkable man, and our relationship was one of the most significant of my life. The first I became aware of him was one of those minor, almost inconsequential incidents that somehow changed the course of events."

What exactly happened?

"The memory remains vivid, as though it happened only yesterday. It was during one of those grand court ceremonies where every detail must be flawless, from the powdered wigs to the intricate embellishments on our uniforms. I was in full ceremonial attire, and every detail was meticulously arranged — or so I thought. However, I felt an odd sense of unease, a nagging awareness that something was amiss. Suddenly, I realised what it was. The hilt of my sword was missing the decorative tassel that should have been there, an essential part of the uniform. A wave of embarrassment washed over me. How could I have overlooked such an important detail? In a court where appearances are everything, such a mistake would not go unnoticed.

As if summoned by my distress, Grigory Potemkin appeared. I'd seen him before among the many officers who served in my court, but he had never stood out to me until that moment. He was tall and broad-shouldered, with a keen, intelligent gaze that saw more than most. And, as it turned out, he had seen my error. Without a word, he approached me, his steps confident yet respectful, as though he were approaching not just a monarch but a woman in need. Reaching into his coat with a hint of a smile, he produced a silk knot, quietly saying, "Your Majesty, I believe this belongs to you."

That must have been such a moving moment, your Majesty.

"When he handed me the knot, our hands touched. Something unspoken passed between us as if he understood the absurdity of it all - the pomp, the ceremony, the endless attention to detail. Yet, he chose not to mock it but to assist me in maintaining the illusion. There was no judgment in his eyes, only a wise look that suggested he found the situation as amusing as I did, though neither of us would ever say so aloud.

From that instant, Potemkin was no longer just another officer in the sea of faces surrounding me. He had marked himself out as someone different. Someone who could see beyond the surface and connect with me on a level few others could. I knew then that he would play a significant role in my life, though I did not know how important it would be. He became my confidant, advisor, and, in many ways, my equal. We had a profound and complicated relationship, full of passion and respect."

I appreciate your honesty, Empress. I know this relationship stood the test of time. He played a vital role in annexing Crimea and expanding your empire in the South. Did you ever grow tired of him, as you did with many others?

"Even after our romantic relationship cooled, we remained close friends and collaborators. I trusted his judgment and valued his insights, and he continued to serve Russia with great distinction until his death. Losing him in 1791 was one of the greatest sorrows of my life."

Finally, Empress Catherine, what do you hope will be your lasting legacy as you look to the future?

"I hope to be remembered as a ruler who truly loved her country and dedicated her life to its progress and prosperity. I wish to be seen as someone who brought Russia closer to Europe, both geographically, culturally, and intellectually. But mostly, I want people to remember that I was a woman who overcame many obstacles to achieve what I did - both as a foreigner in a strange land and as a woman in a man's world. I also want to be known as a ruler who sought to balance the ideals of progress with the realities of power. I will consider my legacy a success if my life and reign inspire others to seek knowledge, be brave in the face of adversity, and strive to improve their society."

The interpreter hands the Empress a beautifully leather-bound volume. "I wish you to have this private publication in memory of our meeting today. It's a book of Enlightenment on the philosophy of my friend Voltaire. I hope you enjoy it."

I stammer my thanks, and the conversation ends as it began. The mysterious door to the chamber swings open as if reading her thoughts, and this remarkable woman of vision, strength, and contradictions passes from my sight.

NOTE: For a more detailed portrait, don't miss Virginia Rounding's masterful Catherine the Great, Arrow Books 2006, and for more about the most extraordinary man that Catherine ever met, enjoy Simon Sebag Montefiore's Prince of Princes, Weidenfeld & Nicolson, 2000.

MARY WOLLSTONECRAFT

1759–1797

A pioneering, unorthodox English philosopher and advocate for women's rights, she is best known for her seminal work, A Vindication of the Rights of Woman. In it, she challenged the prevailing social norms by advocating women's education and equality and laid the groundwork for future feminist movements.

"It is vain to expect virtue from women till they are in some degree independent of men."

Mary Wollstonecraft, A Vindication of the Rights of Woman, 1792

MARY WOLLSTONECRAFT

My conversation with Mary Wollstonecraft is due shortly on this crisp autumn afternoon in 1796. We're due to meet at Thomas Payne's Bookshop, in the heart of London, just off Fleet Street. Mary, who will shortly marry William Godwin, the famous philosopher and political writer, should feel at home here. The shop is well-connected to other intellectual and political venues in the city where radicals, thinkers and philosophers gather.

Payne publishes and sells works by some of the period's most influential writers, including Mary Wollstonecraft. As I await her arrival, I feel slightly tense in anticipation. The shop door swings open, and a quietly confident Mary enters. Her dark hair is elegantly tied back. A few tendrils escape to frame her face. Her eyes scan the room with curiosity. She wears a stylish gown, reflecting her practicality and dignity. She approaches me with a warm smile.

Good afternoon, Mary! It's an absolute honour to meet you. Please do sit down here.

"Thank you. I love this place; it's always so stimulating. Now, tell me, what should we discuss today? I'm keen to share my thoughts on many issues that matter to me."

Can we start with your book Vindication of the Rights of Woman and what made you write it?

'Vindication' was born from sheer frustration and hope. In both law and society, women are still essentially treated as secondary to men. Seeing the widespread limitations imposed on women led me to challenge that status quo. My book argues for their rights, education, and opportunities."

You've mentioned your firsthand experience of women's limitations, which describes your early life.

"It certainly does. I had a challenging childhood, becoming invisible in a large family of seven children. Although we had a comfortable income, my father was hot-blooded, capricious, abusive and squandered the family's resources. In an increasing period of financial instability, I realised the precarious position of women, especially those without economic independence.

Although I hated my father's brutality, I was somewhat like him, with a ferocious temper and a hatred of restrictions. As he struggled to improve himself, we moved around a lot. We went to live in Hoxton and left my best friend behind. I had to walk alone through the rutted streets and was appalled at what I saw. Apart from the dirt and squalor, there were countless beggars, three lunatic asylums and several workhouses for people in desperate poverty.

At first, I was delighted when I managed to get away from Hoxton to become a lady's companion in Bath. But she was so bad-tempered that I returned home to look after my dying mother. With my sisters and a close friend, we set up a school in London's Newington Green to make a living. It was one of my first attempts to promote the importance of education for women. The venture didn't thrive, and when my dear friend died, I didn't have the heart to continue. My financial situation was dire, and once the final student left, numerous creditors chased me like furies.

I tried being a governess to pay my way but hated it. To overcome my grief for my lost friend, another suggested: "The world needs to hear your ideas." So, I started putting down on paper how difficult it was for single women to support themselves. This awareness of women's educational limitations also greatly influenced my later writings."

Was this the start of your writing career?

"Yes, that's how it began. I wrote Thoughts on the Education of Daughters, then a novel and a collection of moral tales for children. None, though, helped ease my miserable financial situation. Then, at last, I had some luck. My book, The Education of Daughters, came into the hands of the publisher, Joseph Johnson. He saw potential in my work and asked me to visit him. To my amazement, he offered an incredible amount of money for a new book. Even better, he gave me a generous advance."

What happened next, Mary?

"Johnson's enthusiasm kept me going. I plunged into my first Vindication book, The Rights of Men, as an angry response to Edmund Burke's Reflection on the Revolution in France. He was against the Revolution and the idea of rights for all. I despised what he said and challenged his assumptions. Instead, I argued for the rights of individuals, particularly in terms of political equality and reform. Having finished it, I rushed a copy to Johnson, and his positive reaction convinced me to try to earn a living as a professional writer. That book made me famous. Although first published anonymously, the second edition in 1790 revealed my name. That's when I started working on my follow-up book, A Vindication of the Rights of Woman.

Because of the earlier book and Burke's views on the French Revolution, I decided to visit France. As England and France were on the brink of war, many friends said don't go. Nevertheless, I arrived in Paris to see Louis XV1's trial before the National Assembly. His dignity under such stress impressed me. To my surprise, I even cried when, a month later, I watched him in a hackney coach going to meet his death at the Guillotine.

After difficulties leaving France because of the war, I returned to England to finish my second book, "A Vindication of the Rights of Woman." I unashamedly built on my arguments in the earlier one on men. Also, my previous teaching experiences underlined the terrible restrictions and lack of educational opportunities for women. The second Vindication book revealed how difficult it was for single women to support themselves and pushed for better conditions and women's rights. Two years after I returned from Paris, the new book finally saw the light of day and was well received.

One can't help but feel moved to hear your passion and persistence in writing.

"Thank you, but I wrote to survive emotionally and financially. Writing came trouble-free because, with friends, I'd previously explored my ideas on child-rearing, schools, women, education, and marriage. Thoughts on these filled my head and poured easily onto the page. Equally encouraging, through Johnson's circle, I met influential thinkers like William Godwin and Thomas Paine."

Could you share more about your relationships with people, for example, with Gilbert Imlay, with whom you had your daughter Fanny?

"My relationship with Imlay was complex. We fell in love during the great political upheaval of the French Revolution. Gilbert was an American entrepreneur and adventurer. We had an ardent union but never married. The relationship was fraught with challenges, and when our daughter Fanny was born in 1794, she became a source of strength and motivation when Imlay abandoned me. This led to a dark period in my life, including several attempted suicides. However, such experiences deepened my understanding of women's emotional and social vulnerabilities, further informing my writing.

Recovering from my deep depression, I gradually returned to my literary life. Then, through my publisher's circle of contacts, where I met William Godwin, the famous philosopher and political writer. William and I have an intellectually stimulating relationship in which we deeply respect each other's work and ideas. We both value personal freedom and independence and are trying to create a partnership that rejects our time's rigid and hierarchical norms.

Your trials and achievements are truly remarkable. Until recently, you've continued to travel extensively. Can you say how your travels

shaped your thinking?

"Touring has proved incredibly eye-opening. For example, my time in France during the Revolution was both exhilarating and disheartening. On the one hand, I witnessed the widespread enthusiasm for liberty and equality. But on the other hand, the violence and chaos were thoroughly alarming. Those experiences highlighted the complexities of social change and drove home to me the need for a measured, thoughtful approach to reform. I set out my thoughts in 'An Historical and Moral View of the French Revolution,' which reflected my evolving political philosophy."

Her eyes sparkle with intensity and conviction. Uninvited, a small eves-dropping audience has gathered unobtrusively around us. Like them, I'm entirely engrossed, hanging on to Mary's every word.

Your ability, Mary, to draw insights from such tumultuous times has stimulated so many people. Can you say what are the most enduring lessons from your work?

"A fair question. The most powerful lesson from my work is about the importance of education and equality. The central argument in 'A Vindication of the Rights of Woman' is that women are not naturally inferior to men. They appear that way because they lack access to education. Society dramatically benefits when women are educated and allowed to participate equally in all aspects of life. These principles remain relevant today. The fight for gender equality continues everywhere."

How can women claim their natural rights despite continued male stubbornness and fear of the true power of women?

"You may well ask. Women must first obtain the character of a human being, regardless of the distinction of sex. I'd also say remain steadfast and resilient since the road to equality is long and often fraught with obstacles. But your efforts in educating, advocating, and supporting one another are vital. Remember, every step forward, no matter how small, contributes to a greater cause. And always, always believe in the fundamental worth and potential of every individual, regardless of gender."

Thank you, Mary, for sharing some of your incredible journey. I am sure your message about women will continue to resonate and empower.

"It's been a pleasure reflecting on and sharing these experiences." As Mary rises to go, the small, uninvited group around us breaks into warm, respectful applause. I find it hard to refrain from applauding, too, as this remarkable woman leaves, returning to her struggles.

NOTE: Wollstonecraft's story is one of fierce independence, groundbreaking ideas, and profound personal struggles. As a writer, philosopher, and early feminist, Mary challenged the traditional views of women's roles. She strongly advocated for women's rights to education, autonomy, and intellectual equality. Her insistence on the importance of rationality, moral development, and equal access to education was revolutionary. What Wollstonecraft stood for continues to influence modern feminist thought.

Mary's life and ideas have left an indelible mark on the intellectual landscape of the 18th and 19th centuries and beyond. She married William Gordon in 1797 and died from complications the same year while giving birth to her daughter, also called Mary. Sadly, Wollstonecraft never saw her second daughter, Mary Shelley, grow into the literary giant and author of Frankenstein.

Charlotte Gordon's Romantic Outlaws, Windmill, 2015, is a detailed, well-researched portrait of mother and daughter and an enjoyable read.

MARIE TUSSAUD

1761-1850

The French artist and sculptor Marie Tussaud was renowned for creating lifelike wax figures. She founded the famous Madame Tussaud's wax museum in London, which showcased historical figures and celebrities. Her work popularised wax sculpture, making it a significant art form. Her legacy endures through the expansion of her museum into various cities worldwide and the attraction of millions each year.

"I became acquainted with the art of wax modelling through a misfortune. But I turned it into a success."

Marie Tussaud A Life in Wax, Susan Vernon, 2004

MARIE TUSSAUD

After travelling with her exhibits for several decades, Madame Marie Tussaud opened her first permanent venue on a short-term lease in Baker Bazaar in 1835. This famous London venue hosts shops, exhibitions, and events and is also ideal for public gatherings. I'm looking forward to meeting a marketing genius whose exhibits in numerous cities around the world continue to attract vast numbers of visitors.

I am shown into a modest room in a rented house near the new permanent exhibits. Marie Tussaud is already seated at a small table, sipping what looks like ordinary water. This year, in 1842, she is over eighty and looking precisely like some of her famous portraits, in which she combines liveliness with a severe expression. Large, rounded glasses accentuate her appearance, and she wears a generous, old-fashioned shawl over her shoulders.

Hello, Madam. It's most kind of you to agree to this conversation with me. I know how busy you are.

"Happy to oblige Monsieur. I'm never too busy to discuss my many-travelled exhibits and their exciting history."

Let's briefly touch on your early days. Is it true you were required to reproduce wax figures of recently executed aristocrats? And, more ominously, were you warned you'd lose your own head if you refused?

After sipping from her glass, Marie chuckles softly: "Ah, that story has followed me for years. While it sounds dramatic, there's some truth to it. As an artist, I lived briefly in the Palace of Versailles. When the revolution began, and the guillotine was so busy, I found myself in a precarious position. Having fallen under suspicion, I was put in prison, possibly facing execution. However, my known ability to create lifelike figures in wax won the attention of some rather dangerous individuals. In those chaotic days after the Reign of Terror began, there was a morbid fascination with the heads of those guillotined. Many executed were high-profile figures - aristocracy, nobles, and even royalty.

The revolution leaders requested or instead demanded that I make death masks from the severed heads of specific individuals. These masks were often displayed as trophies or symbols of victory over the old regime. Yes, I do vividly remember being told, in no uncertain terms, that my head would meet the same fate as those executed if I refused. It was hardly a request one could easily decline."

How on earth, Madam, did you manage to carry out such work under those circumstances?

"It was indeed horrifying. Those executed whose heads I had to model in wax were often previous acquaintances, and some were even friends. But in those days, survival was paramount. So, to keep going, I focused on my craft. As much as possible, I mentally detached myself from the grim reality. I saw it as my duty to survive. With little room for sentiment, I did what was asked of me. No matter how tragic the situation, I had to block it out."

I understand. Were there many notable figures you were asked to reproduce in such circumstances?

"Oh, yes. Many of the victims of the Revolution were prominent figures. Marie Antoinette, for example, was one. I had to create her death mask, which was a terrible moment for me. I had met her years before, in far happier times, when I was commissioned to create her wax portrait. Holding her bloodied, severed head in my hands was a stark reminder of how drastically the world had changed."

How did that experience affect your view of your work?

"Profoundly. My work during the Revolution was not the kind of art I had envisioned when I started. But it was part of my new reality. It deepened my sense of history and mortality. After the Revolution, I continued creating wax figures but carried the memory of those terrible days. I realised life's fragility and how power and status can vanish instantly. This made me all the more determined to preserve history through my figures, not just as likenesses but as stories frozen in time."

It's remarkable how you survived and turned your suffering into something more positive and enduring.

"Those early years taught me resilience and, as I say, the vital need to preserve historical moments. My later exhibitions included many figures from the Revolution and its aftermath. It was crucial to remember the grandeur and the terror of those times. My Chamber of Horrors, for example, is a direct result of that period. However frightful, preserving those moments was a way to confront history's brutality while presenting it as a lesson for future generations."

You undoubtedly did that, turning that grim chapter into a way of keeping history alive for so many people.

"It's always been my goal. To preserve history in wax, to give people a chance to look into the eyes of those who shaped our world, for better or worse. Though my activity during the Revolution was awful, it has become part of my life's work, and I believe it was necessary. If not for myself, then for the sake of posterity."

Thank you for sharing that with me, Madam Tussaud. While I've heard a little about your early years, can you explain how you first got into wax modelling?

"Ah, it feels like a lifetime ago. I was just a girl living in Strasbourg, France, born there in 1761. My father died when I was very young, and my mother and I were left to make our way in the world. Wanting a better life, mother moved to Berne, Switzerland. Fortune arrived for us in the form of Philippe Guillaume Mathe Curtius. Though he practised as a doctor, Philippe had an unusual talent."

This was Curtius, the wax modeller?

"The same. At first, he made anatomical models for medical use. But something was compelling about his skill and his passion for precision. Soon, visitors came to see his creations and increasingly began asking for more, not just bones and muscles but faces and expressions. And that's where I came in. My mother became his housekeeper, and we moved into his home. I was captivated by this work.

Imagine a child watching this master take nothing but wax and create something so real, so full of life. It fascinated me. I'd stand for hours watching him sculpt, and soon, he noticed my genuine interest."

And he taught you how to do what he did?

Nodding slowly: "Curtius was kind though strict in his way. He believed in accuracy and in capturing the finest details. He began by showing me how to shape small things, like hands, ears, and the curve of a smile. It was meticulous work, but I adored it. Most of all, I loved that something could be captured forever, frozen in time, almost immortal.

I was 15 when I made my first wax figure, a model of the philosopher Voltaire, which helped showcase my early talents. My mother, of course, was thrilled. Curtius offered us stability and a future. With his growing exhibit success, Curtius moved us to Paris in the late 1760s. Leaving Berne's rustic charms, a city of clogs, lederhosen, and women in plaits, for the sophistication of Paris was a significant change."

It must have been exhilarating.

"Paris was a different world altogether. It was vibrant and alive with ideas, art, and politics. It was exciting and terrifying. I was plunged into a society where noble women wore wide-hooped skirts, towering wigs, and shoes designed not to be walked in. Curtius opened his exhibition there, and I assisted him full-time, working on the figures that would fill his displays. The city was intoxicating but also harsh."

Harsh in what way?

Sighing deeply: "To anyone naïve, Paris could be extremely nasty. A revolution was brewing, though I didn't see it then. There was unrest and much cruelty. This was no place for weaklings, and it forced me to grow up quickly. For example, I rapidly learned the art of observation, how people moved, and when their faces revealed their true feelings. That observation skill would serve me well later in life, but as a young girl, I found it daunting. I also learned the art of keeping one step ahead, of anticipating and sustaining public interest.

Paris taught me that nothing in life is permanent, not the faces we wear or the lives we live. Seeing the rise and fall of great men and women, some immortalised in wax by my own hands, taught me resilience. Curtius always said, 'Art is both survival and legacy.' And he was right. Those early years shaped me into who I am today.

Curtius revealed every part of the modelling process and shared the secret formulas for tints that create human skin tones. When he died in 1794, he left me his wax collection, including many death masks. Later, I married a civil engineer, Francis Tussaud, and though our marriage was not happy, I had two sons. With France in turmoil and my marriage strained, I moved to England with my sons. Once safely here, I began exhibiting the wax models I'd inherited. There were many opportunities to show them since England was renowned for countless fairs and shows of people peddling exotic experiences, though most were terrible."

Faced with all that competition, Madam, what did you do?

"I developed ways to promote and publicise what I had to offer and create drama that attracted the public. Some of what I did in those early days drew directly from my mentor Curtius. Soon, though, my imagination was running riot. I became an expert at making my name and my shows widely discussed.

You were up against many other ways to create realism, such as animations, automatons, robots, and ventriloquism. Yet, your wax models - your art - endured and outlasted many of those. Why do you think that is?

"Good question. Fascination with machines that move has always been there. People love the idea of creating life, don't they? Something that can move, blink, respond. I saw it myself, even in the days of Curtius, little mechanical wonders — clockwork figures, automata — that could wave a hand or turn their head. But my wax models, well… they did something different.

No matter how impressive, machines are still machines. They move, yes, but it's usually a movement you can predict and one that lacks a soul. A machine can mimic, but it cannot feel. My figures don't move, but they "breathe." Wax captures something that motion can't. It freezes the essence of a moment. The tension in a jaw, the glint of an eye, the curl of a lip. Those are not things that gears and cogs can animate.

Wax allows for intimacy. When you stand before one of my figures, you're not just seeing a likeness but standing face-to-face with history itself. You can study every feature and detail without the distraction of movement. You can reflect, and I believe people connect in that stillness. It's not just about seeing life — it's about feeling it."

But surely people want something more dynamic? Something… alive?

"They think they want that. People are naturally fascinated by automatons, moving dolls, and now moving images. But what people return to time and again is the desire for permanence, to preserve. Movements fade, and actions pass. But a natural, human face captured in wax — endures. It tells a story without needing to speak or move.

That's why I focus so much on the details, capturing not just likenesses but something of the person's spirit."

It's almost as if you have found a way to make wax speak without words.

Marie laughs softly, her eyes twinkling: "Exactly. A wax figure doesn't have to move. In its stillness, it already holds everything it needs to say. People want to look into the eyes of someone famous or infamous, and in that gaze, they try to understand."

So, is it less about the movement and more about presence?

Nodding slowly: "Yes. Presence, permanence, and the power of silence. In a world full of noise and constant movement, something is captivating about standing before a figure and feeling as if time has stopped. People can look at the currently famous and once famous like Marie Antionette and Napoleon, and it's as if they've been given a moment alone with them."

Madam, your recent creation of Queen Victoria's Coronation scene in 1838 has taken the world by storm. How did you bring this momentous event to such a fantastic life?

"For me, the coronation was not just about creating lifelike wax figures. It was about fully immersing visitors in the grandeur of the event. I wanted them to feel like they were standing in Westminster Abbey on that historic day. Every detail, from the costumes to the scenery, had to be exact to achieve this. Recreating the royal regalia and intricate garments was a labour of love. I invested heavily in securing the finest materials, and many were custom-made.

For example, the Queen's coronation robe mirrored the original with its decadent velvet and embroidered gold thread. My team and I studied hundreds of reference images and historical records to ensure that every stitch, every button, and even the way the fabric fell was accurate. We worked closely with costume historians to make sure it was perfect."

Such dedication. And what about the scenery? How did you manage to replicate the atmosphere of Westminster Abbey so well?

"The scenery is just as important as the figures themselves. I wanted to transport visitors into the heart of the ceremony. I spared no expense to replicate the architecture of the Abbey, from the towering arches to the intricate details of the stonework and stained glass. The lighting was also crucial in capturing the solemn yet happy mood of the occasion. We recreated the natural light filtering through the windows and the flicker of candlelight present on that day. People come to Madame Tussaud for entertainment and to witness history come alive.

Every detail helps to tell that story. Whether it's the glint of a jewel on a crown or the echo of footsteps on the Abbey's floor, these elements build the atmosphere, making the experience memorable. No investment can be enough to generate something of this scale and importance. We found the best artists, costume designers, and architects for the coronation to help bring the scene to life."

How do you feel now that it's all complete and on display?

"It's so satisfying when people react to the scene. It makes all the hard work worth it. My goal has always been to create lasting impressions, and I think we've achieved that with this coronation scene."

You also have an unrivalled reputation for creating current news events and bringing them to life, as you did in the 1841 exhibit showing the historic use of the telegraph to capture fleeing murderers.

"Ah, yes—the telegraph and the capture of the infamous murderer, John Tawell. The use of practical science to bring criminals to justice was unprecedented then, and I wanted to showcase the event, the technology and the tension and excitement surrounding them.

It's so dramatic in so many ways! Imagine! In one town, Tawell killed someone and thought he could escape by boarding a train. But the telegraph, then a brand-new invention, was used to send a message ahead to London, where authorities were waiting for him. I knew a scene capturing that intersection of innovation and justice would fascinate visitors. I wanted to recreate both the tension of the telegraph office and the pursuit of the murderer.

So, we built a multi-part scene. In one part, you see the telegraph operator at his desk, sending the critical message: "A murderer is on the train to London." Every detail of the telegraph equipment had to be accurate. We sourced authentic pieces and recreated others. The operator's expression is urgent, with his hand poised over the telegraph key."

In the other part, I wanted to show the moment of suspense in London. The police are gathered, reading the telegram with furrowed brows, preparing to act. You can see the tension in their stances, the anticipation. Outside the train station, I depicted the constables waiting, with the sense that the killer could arrive at any moment.

To recreate the sense of urgency, the trick was for visitors to feel as if they were right there. We studied the uniforms and station settings to make the scene as realistic as possible. The Telegraph was central to the story, but I also wanted to show the physical chase, the murderer stepping off the train, believing he was free, only to be met by the authorities. His face, frozen in shock, is a critical moment in the scene."

Again, Madame, you've taken enormous trouble ensuring historical accuracy. What role does the telegraph itself play?

"Then the telegraph was revolutionary. I wanted its significance to be clear. We even have the telegraph wires running visibly from the station to the operator's office in the scene. The idea was to show how this small device changed the course of justice, ensuring that no one could escape as easily anymore. Translated into dots and dashes, the message changed everything in those few minutes."

Having settled here in Britain, it must feel strange after so many years of travelling from town to town. How many decades has it been?

"Oh, more than four now. I have carried my figures through revolutions, wars, and across continents. Each town has a new story, and each figure has a memory. But it's difficult for a woman my age to continue like that. The world is changing faster than my legs can carry me. With our new permanent location, it's as if I've closed a chapter, but a new one begins. These figures - they've been my companions. They are more than wax; they are history, stories frozen in time.

And finally, I have given them a home, a stage to speak to the future. This is just the beginning, you see. And now, if you'll excuse me, I've some business to attend to and sadly must finish our talk."

Marie Tussaud is gone almost before I can stammer my thanks for this enthralling conversation. She plunges back to the excitement and grind of making history live again to entertain and delight us.

LADY HESTER LUCY STANHOPE

1776–1839

From being a strict conformist to becoming an audacious rebel, the beautiful and captivating Lady Stanhope lived on her own terms. She dared to defy high society and embark on a life of adventure in the Middle East, often clad in Turkish male attire. In the Orient, Lady Stanhope exerted considerable influence as a political and social explorer of the Eastern Mediterranean. She continues to intrigue and fascinate historians and archaeologists. Her pioneering work on unearthing ancient ruins in Palestine significantly contributed to archaeology.

"...don't you realise that if my will dictates something, neither heaven, air or earth will stop me pursuing it?"

Hester writes to a friend, 1814

LADY HESTER LUCY STANHOPE

Lady Stanhope, an early adopter of a hippie lifestyle, was not just a staunch advocate of feminism but a living embodiment of its principles. Her refusal to conform, coupled with her charm, undaunted spirit and spellbinding conversation, has earned her the comparison to a modern Scheherazade. Her influence on feminism continues to resonate across generations, inspiring and empowering people to this day.

I have arrived at her home in Djourn, a stone-built retreat northeast of Beirut, sometimes known as the Castle of Kharab. This area is dominated by dramatic scenery and impressive Roman remains. Lady Stanhope now refuses entry to all but the most unusual strangers. Despite being preoccupied by her mounting and all-absorbing money worries, she has graciously agreed to talk with me.

As darkness falls, I am ushered into Lady Stanhope's presence. She rises gracefully and most formally from her seat, a picture of elegance. Although surprisingly pale, her face exudes a certain charm, and she's wearing a large turban that adds to her enigmatic persona. Her dress, a mass of fine linen loosely folded and vaguely suggesting a religious robe, adds to her captivating allure.

Lady Stanhope, thank you for being willing to meet with me and talk. I'm curious about many things in your life story, but to start with, please tell me what it was like growing up in such a prominent British family like yours.

"Yes, of course. Well, growing up in the Stanhope household was an absorbing experience. My grandfather, the 1st Earl of Chatham, was Prime Minister, and my uncle, William Pitt the Younger, followed in his footsteps. The atmosphere in which I was raised vibrated with politics and power. By paying close attention to the conversation during mealtimes and when we went shooting or travelling, I learned to navigate the complexities of high society."

When Pitt's mother died in 1803, he asked me to be his hostess. I was delighted and became his confidante, managing his household and acting as his political secretary. Often, I was an intermediary between Pitt and key political figures. Gradually, I learned the subtle art of extracting and providing helpful information. I tell you, the whole experience was better than a formal education!"

Your sharp intellect and personality made you a strong presence on the political scene. So, what drove you away?

"Pitt's death in 1806 marked a turning point. I immediately faced intractable personal and financial setbacks, including losing my home and the political influence I once wielded. My ability to find a new role was constrained by the limitations placed on women. Consequently, I felt a growing sense of restlessness and a desire for adventure."

Was that when you decided to leave England four years later, in 1810?

"Yes, I chose to take the risk of going to the Middle East. I hoped that once there, I would have new experiences. Most of all, it would be a break from the conventional life and the political intrigues during those earlier years with Pitt. So, I decided to leave.

Your adventures are widely known, and I understand Constantinople was your first significant stop abroad. Is that right?

"Yes, Constantinople was mesmerising, visually and what it offered those who chose to live there. The City's grandeur and mix of cultures were unlike anything I'd ever seen, and one truly felt the East's allure. Those early travels filled me with a sense of purpose. They fed an insatiable curiosity, and finally, I accepted the inevitable that the conventional role of a woman in society was not for me.

Living in the Orient made me hungry to see the world, make a mark, and have a life of adventure and independence. The place fascinates me — its history, people, and mysteries. I resolved to stay and experience it all firsthand. Most importantly, I wanted to openly challenge the limited boundaries set for women at that time.

This seems like a good moment to share something about your famous shipwreck and how it led to your legendary entrance into Palmyra. It's said you were seeking lost treasures and hidden knowledge.

"You shouldn't pay too much attention to rumours and speculation! I left Constantinople in a traditional Greek fishing boat on my way to the exotic shores of the Levant. We were halfway to Alexandria when we faced gale-force winds and swelling waves. Belatedly, I realised I should have taken a larger boat. Our crew struggled to maintain control. Sails flapped wildly, huge waves crashed over the bow, and the vessel heaved and groaned. After fighting the surging sea for four hours, the boat failed. Still, we managed to land from a small boat on a stony beach near the historical city of Sidon, one of the oldest continuously inhabited cities in the world and not far from Beirut. We lost everything but luckily, we escaped with our lives.

What a disaster. What happened next?

Well, I felt oddly purified by the experience. I shaved my hair and then tackled the problem of what to wear. I rejected the idea of European clothes, and wearing Greek clothes was political madness then. Dressing as a Turkish woman would not work because I could not be seen as speaking to a man. There was nothing left for it but to dress as a Turkish male. If I ever look good in anything, it's in Asiatic dress. In my borrowed Turkish clothes, high-waisted embroidered jacket, kidskin boots and a turban, I confused villagers who sometimes mistook me for a boy.

Comfortable at last, I set my sights on going to the ancient city of Palmyra to see the ruins of Queen Zenobia's city among the date palms of the Syrian desert. Everyone, though, warned me about the great dangers of journeying through the Bedouin territory. To protect me, the local Pasha insisted I should go with a large troop at my expense. Since the Bedouin despised the Pasha through whose land I had to travel, I had to avoid his offer of help. By various dodges, I left without an escort and eventually reached the ancient city of Palmyra, northeast of Damascus. This city is set in an oasis called the "Bride of the Desert," highlighting its beauty and importance as a trade hub."

Tell me about your famed entry to Palmyra, which sounds incredible.

The local Sheikh and some three hundred warriors swarmed out to meet me. Some were naked; others wore loin cloths studded with cowry shells and amulets. As I rode down the central street with its many columns towards a monumental arch, I was welcomed in an ancient manner like a victorious Arab Queen. I earned their trust and admiration by adopting the Bedouins' customs and way of life. They could hardly believe that I rode horses and camels and happily lived in the desert with them. Deep integration into the Bedouin positioned me as a political intermediary among the tribes. That was a familiar role in which I excelled when supporting Pitt. I met with sheikhs and leaders to discuss alliances and regional politics, and I also learned to cast horoscopes."

You had an amulet too, didn't you?

"Yes, I still do. While exploring a hidden temple once, I met some locals who were initially wary of my presence. Yet, when I revealed my amulet to them, they recognised it as a symbol of an ancient protective deity, and their whole attitude shifted. During my travels, when faced with the unknown, I often hold it and recite incantations I've learned from the soothsayer who sold it to me. This practice may seem dubious, but it calms my fears, sharpens my intuition, and guides my encounters. It's more than a talisman; it puts me in touch with my natural resilience. Look, I still wear it." From her clothing Lady Stanhope pulls out the talisman to show me. It's a delicate green stone on which many mysterious symbols are carved."

What an intriguing and beautiful object. Thank you for showing it to

me. And how else has dressing in local costume helped?

"Dressing like this helps me navigate social norms and win authority and acceptance. This would be harder to achieve in traditional Western women's attire. Let me give you an example. While travelling through a bustling market in a nearby town in my Turkish attire, I engaged with local merchants one day. The vibrant colours of my outfit — a flowing kaftan adorned with intricate patterns—blended seamlessly with the rich fabrics and spices surrounding me.

As I approached a stall filled with herbs, spices and dried fruits, the merchant, an elderly wise man, looked me up and down. Expecting to see a foreign woman, he was surprised to see a figure dressed like a local. When I greeted him in Arabic, my accent still reflected my British upbringing. But it was good enough to show respect for his culture, and his eyes widened in surprise.

"Ah! A traveller who understands our ways!" he exclaimed. We began to discuss the spices, and I shared my admiration for their unique qualities. My knowledge and enthusiasm impressed the merchant, who was accustomed to dealing with less informed customers. As our conversation deepened, I spoke of my travels and the stories I'd heard about the ancient trade routes connecting their lands to far-off places like India and China. Intrigued, this merchant invited me to taste some of his finest offerings, such as exotic saffron and fragrant cardamom.

Throughout the market, word spread of the strange woman in male attire who spoke their language and appreciated their goods. A small crowd gathered wherever I went, captivated by my stories and how I commanded attention without demanding it. I negotiated a deal for spices, not just for me but for the local school, to support their efforts in educating children.

By the end of the day, I left the market with a bounty of spices, newfound friendships, and respect from the locals. My choice of attire facilitated my interactions. It symbolised my adventurous spirit and underlined my deep connection to the region. It proved that sometimes, the best way to bridge cultures is through understanding and shared respect."

After many more travels and adventures, Lady Stanhope, you've finally settled in this mountainous region of Lebanon. What drew you here, and what has your life been like?

"The remoteness gives me the solitude and independence I need. I am passionate about it, and here, I can live my admittedly somewhat eccentric and independent life. I adhere closely to local customs and attire, and I'm widely known as a mystic and a leader, respected by the local Druze population.

Lebanon captivated me with its beauty and its strategic location. So, I converted an abandoned monastery into my present home. Before the foundation stone was even laid, I had a complete mental picture of how it should be. The locals now call it "The Fortress". I have my own form of governance and hospitality, blending elements of Western and Eastern cultures."

I've only been here briefly, but your Fortress feels spacious and presumably has plenty of rooms for your visitors.

"Not only that. I even have a secret entrance with a latticed screen through which I can observe visitors in my salon without being seen! Life here has been both confronting and rewarding. Until recently, I managed a large household of staff, engaged in local politics, and hosted travellers and dignitaries worldwide. It's been a life of autonomy and influence, far removed from the constraints of European society."

Can you tell me how your views on religion and spirituality evolved?

"There's no simple answer to that. My experiences in the Middle East have profoundly affected my spirituality. I have been immersed in a beautiful mosaic of beliefs and practices that have broadened and deepened my understanding. While I maintain my Christian faith, I have a deep respect for Islam and other religions. This spiritual evolution is part of who I am and my approach to life."

And what legacy do you expect to leave behind, Lady Stanhope?

"I hope it's one of courage and defiance. I want to be remembered as a woman who broke barriers and lived a life of purpose and adventure. My story shows what can happen if one refuses to be confined by societal expectations."

Your life, courage and refusal to be what's expected continue to inspire many.

"You are kind to say so. I only wish I had the energy left to cast your horoscope. I am so glad you came; it's been a pleasure sharing my story with you; there are so few people left with whom I can do that."

NOTE: Lady Stanhope's life was an incredible blend of adventure, political intrigue, and cultural exploration. Her determined independence and pioneering spirit remind us of the importance of forging our own paths. After a life marked by adventure, she became known for her eccentricities and strong personality. By the end of her life in 1839, she faced significant personal challenges, including financial difficulties and health problems. Her once-prominent social standing had diminished, and she lived in virtual isolation.

While much has been written about her extraordinary life, one of the best and most accessible accounts is Star of the Morning by Kirsten Ellis, Harper Press, 2008

DOCTOR JAMES BARRY

1789-1865

Margaret Ann Bulkley, known during her lifetime as Doctor James Barry, was a pioneering military surgeon in the British Army. Throughout her career, she lived as a man to practise medicine. Barry made valuable contributions to medical science, including one of the first successful caesarean sections when the woman and child survived. Barry was appointed to the top of the medical tree as the Inspector General, equivalent to a lieutenant colonel, and the first woman to rise to this rank in the British Army. The Doctor's Army Commission, signed by Queen Victoria, still exists.

"I have no patience with the conventionality that insists women should not do what men do."

Dr James Barry: A Woman Ahead of Her Time by Janice Blake, 2004

DOCTOR JAMES BARRY, BORN MARGARET ANN BULKLEY

It is 1858, and Doctor James Barry, currently on leave and staying in London, has recently been appointed Inspector-General of Hospitals in Canada. It Is one ot the highest-ranking medical appointments in the British Army, overseeing medical services and health policies.

We're due to meet at the impressive Horse Guards in Whitehall, the headquarters of the British Army Medical Department. The nation is facing multiple conflicts globally, making this a testing time. Immaculately dressed soldiers with polished buttons gleaming in the sunlight salute me as I enter the parade where the Changing of the Guard ceremony occurs daily.

A uniformed cadet guides me through the hallowed halls to a quiet room with two polished upright chairs, in one of which Doctor Barry sits. On rising to greet me, I am surprised at the doctor's size, only about five feet or 1.52 meters. Despite delicate features, a youthful face, and short hair, the Doctor has an unmistakable air of authority and confidence. A flawless dark blue military-style coat with gold braid and epaulettes further implies high status.

Thank you for fitting me into your busy schedule, Doctor. Please be assured that I fully understand the extreme importance of everything here remaining confidential for the foreseeable future.

Doctor Barry offers a slight nod of approval: "Yes, I accept what you are saying. So welcome; where would you like to start our talk today?"

Let's start at the beginning. You were born in Cork, Ireland, as Margaret Ann Bulkley in 1789. Is that correct?

At the sudden mention of her greatest secret, Doctor Barry flinches imperceptibly. However, after at least a minute of silent contemplation that I feel might never end, the Doctor finally nods and continues without hesitation.

"You are correct. But since you are so well-informed, you will also know I only talk about these things to a select few. So, where shall we start?"

Can you tell me about your early years and how you pursued a medical career despite the barriers?

"As you say, I did indeed face many obstacles. My earlier life was filled with both hardship and opportunity. In particular, my father's financial troubles left our family in dire straits."

He was sent to prison for debt, wasn't he, Doctor Barry?

"Yes, but my mother's determination to survive set me on my path. She was a remarkable woman, resourceful and tenacious. After my father's imprisonment, my mother and I moved to London, where we lived with my uncle, James Barry, a celebrated artist and professor. With his connections and the encouragement of forward-thinking individuals like General Francisco de Miranda and Doctor Edward Fryer, the impossible idea of me becoming a doctor took root."

Such a step must have seemed entirely out of the question then.

"It certainly was, and it explains why, to become a doctor, I reluctantly concluded the only way forward would be to live as a man. Without that, I could never have hoped to achieve my ambitions. Women are barred from formal medical education and professional practice. With the active support of my mentors, though, I took on the identity of James Barry. It wasn't just a disguise; it became my life. I enrolled at the University of Edinburgh Medical School in 1809, and my journey began there.

Later, I applied to be a regimental assistant surgeon, paying five shillings to be entered on the list of candidates at the Royal College of Surgeons in Lincoln's Inn Fields. In great trepidation, I later returned for the examination. With several other nervous candidates, I waited many hours before there came a booming announcement: "Doctor James Barry, please", and I found myself before eight important medical scrutineers."

Given your acquired male identity, was it daunting to be under such intense scrutiny?

"You'd think so, wouldn't you? Most of them barely gave me a glance as they carried on talking. Later, they examined in pairs, one quizzing me on surgery and the other on anatomy. The rest watched or entirely ignored the proceedings."

It still sounds scary. Did you struggle with their medical questions?

"Not at all. I'd had far more rigorous oral examinations when I trained in Edinburgh. I passed these in London easily, paying two extra guineas for my certificate as a prospective regimental assistant surgeon."

It must have been a memorable moment. What were some of the most significant difficulties in maintaining your disguise?

"Ah, you want to hear of my trials! Disguising myself as a man has not been easy. Every day means striking a careful balance between scrutiny and survival.

Men's clothing, for instance, isn't just a uniform; it's a constraining suit of armour. Binding my chest is excruciating yet necessary. I also need my movements to be convincingly masculine. There can be no delicate gestures or graceful steps. I adopt a confident stride and a firm handshake. While these come naturally to most men, I have had to cultivate them consciously."

What about your social interactions and meeting your colleagues daily?

"That has been another labyrinth to navigate. I am constantly under the watchful eyes of colleagues and society. Casual banter about 'manly' pursuits and even sharing a drink requires a steady performance, such as being well-versed in politics and military strategy. That's expected of any man in my position. It also hasn't helped that some of my interests, such as vegetarianism and my little menagerie of half a dozen miniature tan terriers, mark me as eccentric.

Is there one significant challenge that stands out in your mind even now?

"Yes, during my medical training at the University of Edinburgh. That place is fiercely competitive. Being seen as anything less than exceptional would arouse suspicion. I threw myself into my studies, often staying up late into the night, focused on medical texts and practising procedures until they became second nature. My efforts paid off; I graduated with top honours, but the pressure to excel was relentless."

What about the physical examinations of patients?

"Well, I don't do physical examinations now. But when I did them, it meant being close, touching and examining while ensuring no one got too near me. During the most intimate medical procedures, my secret had to remain hidden. I can tell you this: throughout my career, every encounter was a tightrope where a single misstep could prove a disaster and reveal everything.

My military service generally has posed its own set of trials. The life of an army surgeon is gruelling, and the battlefield is no place for hesitation. In the heat of combat, I had to suppress any instinctive reactions that might reveal my true identity. Commanding respect from soldiers and officers alike required a bearing of unwavering authority. In actual combat, I had to be more challenging, braver, and resilient than any of my male counterparts. I was constantly proving that I was more capable."

What a terrible strain. What about simple acts like bathing?

"You're right, this was stressful. When there is no privacy, I bathe secretly, early in the morning or late at night, ensuring I am never seen without my clothes. Constant vigilance is exhausting. But it's the price I pay to live my truth and practise the profession I love. Despite all the difficulties, the rewards are immense. I've improved hospital sanitation and advocated for better patient treatment. Every challenge I've overcome has made me stronger and more determined."

But hasn't this permanent disguise been a constant strain?

"Absolutely and remains so. But it's also a shield allowing me to achieve what would otherwise have been impossible. In the early days, I looked extremely young. One of my first postings was to the military General Hospital in Plymouth. When I reported to the Principal Medical Officer, Joseph Skey, he was shocked by my appearance, protesting to his superior that I was 'a mere boy.' Thankfully, his protest fell on deaf ears. Eventually, a few months later, having seen me at work, he changed his mind about my abilities and gladly accepted me onto his staff."

Besides a youthful appearance, what other difficulties remain?

"Living a double life demands ceaseless vigilance. I must constantly demonstrate my competence as a doctor and not let up on the question of identity. I must forever prove my abilities. Still, I'm settled into my assumed role, and with practice and promotion, my disguise has gradually played a lesser part in my concerns. What counts is my work to improve hospitals. For example, transforming sanitary conditions, performing surgeries, and advocating for patients have earned me considerable respect."

You are being too modest, doctor. Your contributions to medical science and public health have been groundbreaking. What are you most proud of?

"That's easy! One of my most gratifying successes was the caesarean section I performed in Cape Town in 1826. It was one of the first in which both mother and child survived. I never stop arguing for better nutrition and humane treatment of patients, soldiers, and prisoners. I believe that my efforts have contributed to the broader public health reforms that were desperately needed."

Your passion for healthcare extends beyond medical practice. You're known for your advocacy for marginalised groups. Can you elaborate on that?

"Certainly. Working in various British colonies exposed me to the harsh realities faced by many marginalised groups, such as enslaved people, prisoners, and the impoverished. Everyone deserves dignity and access to proper medical care. I have never stopped fighting against the mistreatment of the vulnerable. I keep pushing to ensure that medical facilities are accessible to all, regardless of social status."

This commitment has hardly endeared you to those in positions of power.

"No, you're right! My outspoken nature makes me somewhat at odds with the authorities, although I stand by my principles. I am no stranger to conflict in the operating room and the duelling grounds."

Can you talk a bit more about duelling?

"You want some juicy details, eh? Well, my most serious duel happened in 1827 in Cape Town. I faced off against a fellow officer, Lieutenant Edward W. Smith, over a matter of honour. With the sun setting, I stood my ground with my eyes fixed on my opponent. With swords drawn, we proceeded to clash fiercely. We battled away, but the result was more about restoring personal honour than achieving a definitive victory. After exchanging blows and neither of us seriously hurt, we called off the duel and walked away unharmed."

Was there any army criticism of such behaviour or your fiery

temperament?

"Not at all. I was privately commended for my skill and composure under pressure. It solidified my reputation as a capable physician and a man of principle in the long term. My temperament has been both a blessing and a curse. It certainly keeps my colleagues on their toes! My nature drives me to challenge the status quo and fight for what I believe in.

I demand excellence not only from myself but from those around me. While it has led to conflicts, it has also earned me a reputation as someone fiercely dedicated to my profession and my patients. A relentless pursuit of excellence has ultimately defined my career. For example, I am passionate about ensuring proper ventilation, fresh food, clean water, and adequate sanitation facilities. This has made hospitals safer and healthier environments for patients, with reduced infection rates. Perhaps less known is my introduction to the hospitals of detailed patient record-keeping. These help keep track of the effectiveness of treatments over time."

"You've been most frank and open. Perhaps your true identity will emerge someday. I wonder how you feel about such a possibility?

"It's a good question. I accept that the revelation of my true identity may be inevitable someday. I hope it can be delayed for many more years. Living as James Barry is not a deceit but a means to an end. It allows me to fulfil myself in a world that would otherwise confine me. I hope my life can be understood not as a curiosity but as realising my potential, supported by resilience and determination to follow my path."

So, what would you advise future generations, particularly women, aspiring to break gender barriers?

"Persevere. The path won't be easy, that's for sure. Also, never allow social norms to dictate your aspirations. Forge your path with courage and conviction. The world always needs pioneers willing to challenge the status quo, and every broken barrier paves the way for those who follow."

There's a discreet knock on the door, though nobody enters. It's a well-planned signal that our time together has ended. The doctor rises and shakes my hand.

Thank you, Doctor Barry, for sharing your incredible journey.

"It's been a pleasure to share my story freely, and I trust your earlier assurance of confidentiality. There are so few I dare trust with my secret. Goodbye."

NOTE: Doctor Barry's true identity never surfaced during a lifetime of army service. It was only revealed after Barry died in 1865, aged 75, making Margaret Ann Bulkley one of the most intriguing figures in medical history. The sensational revelation about Barry's gender flew around the world and reached many who had known the doctor throughout a distinguished career. Some claimed to have guessed the secret. Others just wondered how on earth a woman had perpetuated such an audacious deception.

Barry's contributions to military medicine were transformative. Some consider him, in advance of Florence Nightingale, to have an even broader vision of rigorous cleanliness standards, reduced infection rates, and mortality among soldiers. Barry's advocacy for humane treatment extended to all patients, regardless of rank, promoting fair and equal care. These initiatives not only improved the immediate welfare of soldiers but set new standards in hygiene and medical practice.

This conversation has benefited from the superb book: "A Woman Ahead of Her Time" by Michael du Preez and Jeremy Dronfield, One World.

MARY SEACOLE

1805–1881

The Jamaican nurse and healer Mary Seacole is celebrated for her remarkable solo efforts during the Crimean War. Despite facing rejection from Florence Nightingale's team, mainly due to racial prejudice, she forged her path. She established her own medical and commercial facility to care for soldiers. Blending traditional Caribbean remedies with Western medicine, Mary offered care and concern, a quality she believed to be of utmost importance in nursing.

"Unless I am allowed to tell the story of my life in my own way, I cannot tell it at all."

Mary Seacole, Wonderful Adventures of Mrs Seacole in Many Lands, 1857

MARY SEACOLE

The hallowed ground of knowledge and history of the British Library's Treasures Gallery is just right for a profound conversation with Mary Seacole. My comfortable Gallery armchair rests beside an impressive mahogany and glass showcase with numerous letters, documents and medals from the 19th century. They all relate to the Crimean War, a time intimately familiar to Mary Seacole.

Mary arrives, her upright bearing immediately attracting my attention. She's wearing a dark, tailored dress with subtle embellishments, reflecting her mixed heritage. Briefly, we observe each other out of curiosity. Eager to begin our conversation, I break the silence.

It's an immense privilege to speak with you today, Mrs Seacole. You've had such adventures. Thank you for making the time to be with me today.

Offering a much-weathered hand, the skin tightly drawn, Mary's firm grip suggests continued vibrancy: "Well, here I am. It's good we can get together, and you want to hear about my travels and activities. No doubt you've read my book about them?"

Of course, "The Wonderful Adventures of Mrs. Seacole in Many Lands". It describes your amazing life well.

"I am so pleased you like it. What more would you like to know?"

Can you share a bit about your early life and what inspired you to pursue nursing?

"Well, I was born Mary Grant in a small Jamaican hamlet called Haughton, about 80 miles west of Kingston, at the start of the 1800s. My mother was a free black woman and a traditional healer, and my father was a Scottish soldier. I grew up surrounded by my mother's health practice."

Is that how you learned about herbal medicine and the importance of caring for the sick?

"Yes, I enjoyed watching her prepare her holistic Jamaican medicines and started imitating her nursing skills. While playing with my dolls, whatever disease was most prevalent in Kingston, my doll soon contracted it. I suppose it was inevitable that the ambition to become a doctress early took root in my mind."

What was it like living in Kingston at the start of the century?

"I don't mind confessing that the century and I were both young together, and there were many unpleasant things about it then. Let's leave it at that."

I understand. But could you explain how your mixed heritage influenced your life and work?

"I am proud of that heritage, but it has been both a blessing and a trial. Scottish heritage gave me a degree of social mobility many black Jamaicans didn't possess. However, there was also significant racial prejudice, especially when I travelled. But my mother taught me to be proud of who I am and to use my knowledge and skills to help others, regardless of race or background."

Your husband was from a different background, I believe?

"Yes, Edwin Horatio Hamilton Seacole was a white man from an interesting family with complex connections to Lord Nelson. We married in Kingston when I was thirty-one in 1836. We had a good, though short, life together for eight years. This included setting up a shop selling food and herbal remedies. But Edwin was in poor health, and I nursed him until he died in 1844."

After that, you journeyed extensively, but what caused you to leave Jamaica and seek opportunities abroad?

"Growing up with a strong sense of adventure and a desire to expand my knowledge, I began to indulge in a longing to travel. That urge will probably never leave me while I have health and vigour. My first significant journey was when I was about sixteen, accompanying some relatives to London.

Four years after my husband died, and during the gold rush in Panama in 1848, I decided to go there and help care for cholera patients. That and each of my many later journeys proved to be learning experiences that broadened my medical knowledge and skills."

What was Panama like and what did it teach you?

"Panama was a frontier country with an almost powerless government. I can tell you it was a dangerous and cruel environment with rampant disease. Cholera was particularly devastating, and many people were too afraid to treat the sick. But I felt a duty to help. I combined what I'd learned about European medicine to treat patients and used a detailed knowledge of traditional remedies. This was difficult yet gratifying to see so many people recover."

Your most famous contributions, though, came during the Crimean War. How did you end up there?"

"When I heard about the terrible conditions faced by British soldiers in Crimea, I felt compelled to offer my services. Before my departure, I approached the War Office in Britain to volunteer as a nurse. Florence Nightingale was organising nurses to go to Crimea, and I asked to join her team but was turned down through an element of racial prejudice. But I refused to be deterred. Even though it was a demanding journey, I arranged to go to Crimea independently.

That was so bold of you. When you got there, did you set up a hospital right away?

"No. Instead, I started what I called the "British Hotel" near Balaclava, caring for soldiers on the battlefield. My approach was strictly hands-on, with close interactions with soldiers.

What exactly was this hotel? Can you describe it to me?

"As I explained in my book, this was a part-store, clinic, and canteen. Somehow, I had to attract money so my soldiers could get hot food, medical care, and some comfort away from the front lines. Occasionally, under fire, I even treated soldiers on the battlefield. It was such a brutal environment, and I wanted to provide a sense of home and humanity."

How did the soldiers and other medical staff receive you?"

"The soldiers called me 'Mother Seacole' and were deeply grateful for my care. They appreciated my warmth and kindness, which was otherwise in short supply. Some medical staff were sceptical at first, but few could deny the positive impact of my work. Over time, many came to respect and admire my dedication and skills."

Can you share some other challenges you experienced while working in Crimea?

"The conditions were atrocious, with constant danger from shellfire, inadequate supplies, and extreme weather. Again, I faced racial prejudice, but I refused to let this hinder my work. The needs of the soldiers were always my top priority.

Meeting the constant demands of the British Hotel was often beyond my strength. I suffered from overwork, hardly slept, and rarely had time to eat. There was so much catering to do, with joints of meat to cut, chickens to pluck and gut, pastry to mix, cakes to bake, and coffee to brew. Customers would begin arriving by seven in the morning because the hotel was well-placed, near the road from Balaclava up to Lord Raglan's HQ and the camps."

Could you not get any help, Mary?

"Even with the help of a few boys, two black cooks, some Turks, and others in search of employment, it was still difficult to keep up with demand from my customers. You see, my cooking time was forever interrupted by requests to bandage wounds and mix medicines. My working day rarely ended before eight in the evening when we stopped trading.

When officers knew they were going into action the following day, anticipating their possible death, many would ride down to my Hotel to enjoy an excellent meal and to cheer themselves up. They also said goodbye to me because they couldn't do so to their dear ones at home. There was nothing in the world I wouldn't do for them.

I covered several miles each day before sunrise to reach and help the wounded. Army pickets often tried to stop me from approaching the action. But once they knew who they were dealing with, most let me pass. When I was regularly under fire, people called out anxiously to me, "Lie down, mother, lie down, and I would be forced to dive for cover."

What stress you must have been under. Did you ever doubt your essential function there in Crimea?

"Never. No, never. I knew I was needed. Every single day told me that."

You mentioned Florence Nightingale earlier. What was your relationship with her?

"Our paths crossed occasionally. Florence Nightingale was an exceptional woman and made vital contributions to nursing. However, our approaches were very different. She focused on large-scale organisation and sanitation. In contrast, I provided more direct, hands-on care. Although there was some tension, largely due to the prejudices of the time, we were both committed to improving the care of soldiers."

After the war, what was it like coming back to civilian life?

"Challenging. Having spent all my resources on the war effort, I returned to England penniless. Thankfully, the soldiers I cared for remembered me fondly, and there was a public campaign to support me. Eventually, I wrote my autobiography, which helped raise funds to share my story with a broader audience."

Your autobiography is riveting. Unsurprisingly, it became a bestseller. Please tell me, Mrs Seacole, what message did you hope to convey through your book?

"I'm not much of a writer. But, I wanted to share my experiences and highlight the contributions of women in fields like medicine and nursing, especially by women of colour. I felt I had a duty to inspire others to pursue their dreams despite obstacles. While my life has been filled with challenges, it has also been bursting with incredible opportunities to make a difference."

There is no doubt your work has had a lasting impact. How do you now view your legacy?

"I am truly honoured that my work is still remembered and appreciated. Recognising the contributions of all who care for the sick and wounded, regardless of their background, is important. I hope my story arouses concern, encourages resilience, and stirs people to have the courage to overcome adversity."

Finally, what advice would you give aspiring nurses and healthcare workers today?

"Stay committed to your patients and your principles. This world will always need compassionate and skilled caregivers. Learn as much as possible, stay curious, and never let prejudice or hardship deter you from your mission. Your work is invaluable, and every act of kindness can make a significant difference."

Thank you, Mrs Seacole, for sharing some of your demanding and rewarding journey with me. Your life and legacy continue to uplift countless people worldwide.

"Thank you. I've enjoyed sharing my story, and I hope it encourages others to pursue their passions and positively impact their communities."

60

NOTE: Mary Seacole's indomitable spirit, contributions to nursing, and lasting impact of her work are a moving reminder of the power of resilience and compassion in adversity. In 2004, for the initial launch of the 100 Great Black Britons campaign, Mary Seacole was voted the Greatest Black Briton of all time. The Mary Seacole Trust exists to educate and inform the public about Mary Seacole's life, work, and achievements (https://www.maryseacoletrust.org.uk/).

A nationwide appeal supported by thousands of individuals, the military, and major corporations resulted in a statue of Mary at St Thomas' Hospital in London, opposite the Houses of Parliament, in June 2016. For a riveting account of Mary Seacole's life as perhaps the most famous Black woman in Victorian Britain, see Helen Rapport's insightful and well-researched book In Search of Mary Seacole, Simon & Schuster, 2022.

HARRIET TUBMAN

c. 1822–1913

Harriet Tubman, an American abolitionist and political activist, demonstrated unparalleled courage when she escaped slavery and personally led hundreds of enslaved people to freedom via the 'Underground Railroad.' Known as "Moses" for her fearless rescue missions, she also served as a Union spy and nurse during the Civil War and became a symbol of courage and freedom.

"I freed a thousand slaves; I could have freed a thousand more if only they knew they were slaves."

Tubman

HARRIET TUBMAN

To meet Harriet Tubman in the summer of 1903, I am now in Auburn, New York. This is where Tubman has settled, after her remarkable efforts before, during, and after the US Civil War. Now, she's living out her later years in the same modest house where she cared for older people and those in need.

As I reach the top step of her porch, Harriet welcomes me with a wave, taking her place on the nearby wooden rocking chair. This brave and determined woman, now in her 80s, wears simple clothes with a shawl over her shoulders. There's a small table nearby with cornbread and fruit drinks, everyday staples of rural households in Tubman's earlier life."

It's lovely to meet you, Harriet Tubman, and a real privilege. There's so much I want to talk to you about. Can we start with where your personal story began, such as where you were born?

"Thank you kindly, please call me Harriet. I was born on the Eastern Shore of Maryland in 1822 and named Araminta Ross. But most know me by the name I took later—Harriet Tubman. Both of my parents and I were enslaved. Slavery is the next thing to hell.

For years, I harboured dreams of freedom. In my dreams, I soared over fields, towns, rivers, and mountains, like a bird. But always, I came to a great fence or a river, which I attempted to cross. In my dream, there were women in white who would reach out and guide me across. It wasn't until I was about 27 that I felt the call to seize my freedom and escape to the North.

You must have done this with a great deal of trepidation.

"You're right. I realised that such a journey North would be full of dangers. Most frightening were the hoards of brutish bounty hunters on the lookout for escaped slaves. They were paid to track us down, and there would be terrible punishments if caught.

Despite the risks, I fled Maryland alone. In great anxiety, I made my way through the dangerous byways of Delaware and into Pennsylvania. Luckily, I knew some antislavery places dotted around the country where I might get help. One white woman, for example, supported me during the first part of the journey. I moved at night, resting and hiding during the day. Most of my journey was on foot; eventually, I got away and free.

However, I could not rest knowing my family and so many others were still suffering under slavery. So, I began making my way back, returning again and again. I trusted in the Lord to protect me. I also developed skills at evading my pursuers and became increasingly organised."

Voluntarily returning to the South was a terrible risk.

It was a significant risk, but one I was willing to take. In secret, I journeyed back to the South nearly thirteen times, liberating about seventy individuals and leading them to freedom along the clandestine escape routes known as the 'Underground Railroad'.

This, of course, wasn't a real Railroad. Could you describe how it worked?

Indeed, it was not a railroad in the traditional sense. Instead, it was a covert network of routes, homes, and individuals who believed in the inherent right to freedom. The success of the 'Underground Railroad' hinged on the collaboration of all involved. Together, we established a covert system of interconnected 'stations' where fugitive slaves could find refuge on their perilous journey to freedom.

I was what we called a Conductor, but one of many who took part. Our success relied on a combination of roles, each contributing to the larger mission of helping enslaved individuals flee captivity. As Conductors, we often travelled with our "passengers"— the people escaping by night. Conductors knew all about secret routes, forests, rivers, and mountains. They were skilled navigators and could find their way using the stars if necessary."

You became famous for your skill, resourcefulness, and courage in this role. Please tell me more about it.

"In guiding our passengers, we created coded songs and signals and used our instincts to evade slave catchers and bounty hunters. I learned that it was essential that none of my passengers ever returned home through fear. Retreating like that risked exposing the entire network to danger. We Conductors worked with others to avoid capture and relied on Station Masters who offered safe houses or "stations" along the escape route."

It must have been tough for them to become involved this way.

"Certainly, yes. These brave people took terrible personal risks by providing runaways with food, shelter, and protection. If caught harbouring escapees, they could face legal punishment, fines, or even violence. Despite the dangers, our station network stretched across the Northern states and into Canada, which had abolished slavery."

Apart from Conductors and Station Masters, who else helped the railroad function?

"A sensible question. Let me explain. Some people acted as Agents helping to connect enslaved people with Conductors, and they provided information about the best routes. Many were part of the abolitionist movement and maintained communication across state lines.

Those who helped us were called Shareholders. They donated money, food, clothing, and other supplies to support escapees and maintain the secret network. Churches were often vital financial contributors. Especially those linked to the abolitionist movement. Some well-known abolitionists, like Frederick Douglass, supported the Underground Railroad financially."

Tell me about Douglass, who he was, and how he helped your cause.

"He wasn't a Conductor or directly involved in the operation of the Underground Railroad. He was a reliable supporter and worked with us when he could. Douglass, bless him, used his influence to help our movement in several ways. For instance, in his newspaper, the Northern Star, he publicised many moving stories about our cause rather than revealing details of the underground system. He wrote speeches and articles, helped rally public support, and raised awareness about our dangerous work."

Given the constant threat of exposure, secrecy must have been vital. How did you all communicate?

"We often used coded language. For example, the term "station" referred to a safe house, and "freight" or "cargo" referred to the escaping enslaved people. Phrases like "the wind blows from the south today" could signal that fugitive slaves were arriving.

There were also visual cues, such as lanterns hung outside houses or quilts with particular patterns, which could indicate that a home was safe to approach. Spirituals — songs sung by enslaved people — sometimes carried hidden messages. For instance, "Follow the Drinking Gourd" was a secret reference to the Big Dipper constellation, which pointed to the North Star, guiding escapees to freedom.

What about the routes that the "passengers", the escaping slaves, took?

The routes themselves were dangerous and varied, as the enslaved people and their guides had to evade patrols and cross tricky terrain. Some went through cities like Philadelphia, New York, and Boston, while others passed through the Appalachian Mountains or followed rivers. The US 1850 Fugitive Slave Act made it dangerous for escaped slaves to remain in the northern United States. This dreadful law allowed slave catchers to pursue and capture runaways even in free states. Canada became a safer place where U.S. laws didn't apply.

With hindsight, do you know the overall impact of the Railway?

"Numbers are not my strength. But I believe our Underground Railroad helped around 100,000 enslaved people escape between the late 18th century and the end of the Civil War in 1865. Thankfully, during the war, Congress repealed the Fugitive Slave Acts and slavery was officially made illegal at the end of the war.

You were one of its most effective Conductors, and I believe you earned the nickname "Moses" for leading your people to freedom.

"Look, it's nice to be recognised, but please be clear. I wasn't the only one. The Railroad was more than just a pathway to freedom. It became a movement symbolising resistance, solidarity, and the fight for human rights. It relied on the bravery and compassion of many people from all walks of life — black and white, rich and poor, free and enslaved. They were united by a common goal of ending the tyranny of slavery.

You also played a significant role in the Civil War. Can you share what led you to become involved in that fight?

"When war broke out, I realised it was time to do more than lead small groups to freedom. The fight for liberty needed to happen on a much larger scale. So, I worked with the Union Army. At first, I served as a nurse and cook, roles that women were expected to do. Soon, my skills as a scout and spy were recognised, and I became both of them. I knew the South well from all my journeys, which proved valuable to the Union.

For example, I led a successful military raid along the Combahee River in South Carolina in 1863, using leadership and tactical expertise. We managed to free over 700 enslaved people in that single mission."

That extraordinary raid, Harriet, is considered one of the boldest military operations of the entire Civil War. What did that moment

mean to you?"

"I had been freeing people for years in secret, tiptoeing in the shadows. But after that raid—it was out in the open, a declaration. We weren't asking for freedom anymore; we were taking it. To see those men, women, and children step onto the boats, knowing they were no longer enslaved, filled me with pride and peace. It was a day that marked not just the freedom of those 700 souls but the possibility of freedom for many more. That raid showed the world that we were soldiers fighting for liberty."

Harriet, I hope I won't offend you if I ask about something that puzzles me. It's about learning to read and write.

She laughs: "Of course I'm not offended. As you say, I am illiterate; I even sign my name with an X. Strangely, I never got the hang of making sense of written words. But you know I never let it hold me back."

How did you read maps, signs and posters on your perilous journeys?

"It's true I didn't read maps as you would. Instead, I relied on an exceptional memory and a strong understanding of the geography of the areas I travelled to. Landmarks, natural features, and my own experiences helped me to navigate. I also worked with other conductors on the Underground Railroad who could read maps, and I usually memorised routes. I have a keen sense of direction and developed the ability to adapt to changing circumstances. These were all crucial to my success in guiding people to freedom."

Thank you for explaining that. You continued fighting for justice even after the Civil War. Can you tell me about your work in the later years of your life?

"Once the war ended, my family and I settled here at 180 South Street, on the outskirts of Auburn. But I didn't stop fighting. Instead, I worked for the rights of women and older people. I spoke out for the suffrage movement because I believed women should have the right to vote. Women had fought alongside men for freedom, and it was only fair that we should have a say in the laws that governed us."

You were not entirely alone in this struggle, were you? For example, Sojourner Truth was one of your contemporaries. She's known for her powerful speeches and advocacy for abolition and women's rights.

"That's true, I knew her. In Auburn, I also opened my home to those who needed care - the sick, the elderly, anyone who had nowhere else to go. I gave whatever I had because I believed in the power of community and compassion. When I look around, I see that same need for care today, and it reminds me that we all have a responsibility to help others."

You've lived a life of such extraordinary service and sacrifice. Looking back, what do you think is your most satisfying achievement?

"That's hard to say. You see, I didn't do it for glory or recognition. I did it because it was right. When I led people to freedom, I gave them hope. I showed them what it meant to be free, to live with dignity, and to know that they mattered, no matter what the world tried to tell them."

Harriet, your legacy is undeniable. In what ways do you hope your story continues to inspire future generations?

"I want people to understand that freedom isn't free - it requires sacrifice, courage, and a heart willing to do what's right, no matter the cost. I want my story to remind people that one person can make a difference. I was just a small woman, born enslaved, with no education or money. But with faith, I was able to help free hundreds, inspire thousands, and leave behind a legacy of freedom and justice. I want people to look at me or my life story and know that no matter where you start, you can do something great with your life. You can fight for what's right and, in doing so, change the world."

You've touched on the essence of freedom - physical, emotional, and spiritual. What advice would you give to those still fighting for freedom today?

"My friend, the fight for freedom never ends. It may change forms, but it's always there. To those searching for freedom, I say, keep going, trust in your purpose, and remember that even when the world is against you, there's always light ahead. No struggle is in vain if it is for a just cause. And as long as one person remains enslaved, none of us are truly free."

People will face many obstacles along the way, won't they? What would you tell them about that?

"Yes, of course, there'll be obstacles and moments when you want to give up. That's when you have to keep pushing. Fight for those who don't have the strength or voice to fight for themselves.

Your wisdom, resilience, and spirit, Harriet, have shaped not only your time but continue to ripple across history, inspiring generations. What do you hope people will most remember about you?

"Just that I was someone who loved her people. Someone who believed in freedom so deeply that I was willing to risk everything for it. I wasn't a grand leader or a politician. I was a woman who saw injustice and knew in her soul that I must do something. If people can look at my life and see that it's possible to stand up, to act with courage, and to make a difference, then that's enough for me. I did what I could with what I had, and if others do the same, this world will be a much better place."

Thank you, Harriet. Your words are a gift, just as your actions have been crucial for humanity. Your extraordinary contribution will never be forgotten.

"I'm grateful to be remembered. But more than that, I'm rewarded because the work for freedom continues. There's still a long way to go, but we will get there together."

NOTE: Harriet did not see herself as a hero, merely doing the Lord's bidding. Her work was critical to the feminist legacy, reminding us that the fight for freedom is not over. Just before she died peacefully in 1913, she urged the power of persistence: "If you want to taste freedom, keep going."

You may also enjoy Catherine Clinton's well-researched book Harriet Tubman: The Road to Freedom, Back Bay in 2005.

LADY FLORENCE BAKER

1841–1916

As a Caucasian child, Florence Baker fled the Hungarian Revolution in 1848 but was captured and enslaved. About to be sold in a slave market, she was dramatically rescued by her future husband, explorer and adventurer Sir Samuel Baker. Together, they surveyed the Nile, and Florence earned a reputation for her resilience and bravery. The couple retired to Cairo, and after Samuel died in 1894, Florence devoted the rest of her life to preserving his reputation and name.

"I have not come here to ask for anything but to claim what is mine by right."

Florence Baker: The Story of a Female Explorer by Louisa Price, 2001

FLORENCE BAKER

On a hot Egyptian weekday in September 1897, I'm about to enter Florence Baker's home in Cairo. She's lived here alone since the death a few years ago of her famous explorer husband, Sir Samuel Baker. A maid who seems to be expecting me answers the doorbell and escorts me into a pleasantly furnished drawing room adorned with artefacts, tapestries, small statues and numerous souvenirs from the Baker's travels. Despite the warm day, a small fire in the grate adds to the cosy ambience. A large window bathes the room with soft afternoon light. Before I have time to sit down, Lady Florence Baker enters wearing a modest Arabic gown, extends her hand and invites me to sit by the fireplace.

"Welcome. Thank you for coming to Cairo. Please make yourself comfortable. It's not every day that I have a visitor so genuinely interested in my life's journey. I hope you find it worth it! By the way, let's not make this just a formal conversation. So do use my first name."

Thank you for agreeing to see me, Florence. I've read much about your remarkable life and am eager to hear directly from you.

"I'll try and oblige, though much of my existence feels distant, almost otherworldly. Where should we begin? Perhaps with how Samuel and I first met?"

That would be wonderful, Florence, but let's start with you. You have sometimes been called "The Stolen Woman." Do you think that's a fair description?

"Well, to be more accurate, you should say I'm a twice-stolen woman. I was living in a harem in Viddin in the Ottoman Empire after being captured and sold as a child. Much later, I was abducted by Samuel while he was on an expedition exploring."

Can you please talk about the early part of your life?

"Going back, I was born in 1841 and named Florence Barbara Maria von Sass in Nagyenyed, a small market town in Transylvania. It was part of the Austrian Empire with a large Hungarian population. My nurse fled with me, aged about seven or eight, during the 1848 Hungarian Revolution. My entire family was killed, and my nurse fled with me to the apparent safety of Viddin. This town near the Danube River became a refuge during the Hungarian Revolution."

From there, how did you end up in a harem?

"My nurse deserted me or was bribed to hand me to an Armenian slave merchant. He sold me to the harem of the local Ottoman governor, and I was there about seven years. Given my value as a blonde, multilingual Caucasian, I was treated well enough in the harem. Frankly, it's hard to remember all the details, but Harem life was strict yet structured. While there, I learned many new things, including languages, mathematics, and the arts. The woman in charge ensured I was well-trained, though I didn't know she intended to sell me when I was older."

And then came the day you were put up for auction?

"Yes, and it was a terrifying experience. You see, I'd recently received expensive clothes and valuables. Naively, I assumed they were for marriage and that this was how things were done. Little did I know that I was being made ready for sale."

Did you choose these costly clothes, or were you told what to wear?

"I insisted on making my own choice. With the help of the master's favourite concubine, I selected a gorgeous costume in rich blues and greens with bright yellow patterns.

I bet that dress and your blonde hair looked terrific, Florence.

"You're right, it did. Also, I had new yellow boots that fitted tightly around my dainty ankles. I miss those ankles. But they didn't survive my later travels in Africa. On presentation day, several of us from the Harem were assembled in a highly decorated reception room. My friend Fatima and I were placed behind a screen, and I finally realised what was happening. She was taken into the crowded room first. Men started bidding for her, like a cow or a length of cloth. I protested loudly to Ali, my permanent protector in the harem."

He was a eunuch, wasn't he?

Yes, and I loved him like a father. He was devoted to me and gently explained that I would be sold that very day. Given my looks, he predicted there would be plenty of buyers. I grew up in the Harem, which felt like my home. I could hardly take in what was happening and kept shouting in protest: "But I am not a slave. I'm not like the other girls." until I was told severely to stay silent.

The auction was a grim spectacle. Stiff with anger, I was forced to stand alongside the other enslaved people, being assessed as though they were mere commodities. I remember feeling a mix of fear and resignation. Buyers scrutinised us not for our individuality but as property."

Unbearable, Florence. No wonder you were stunned.

"That's putting it mildly. I was in complete turmoil. Mentally, I refused to be treated like an animal for sale. Even though I had no choice but to stand and turn to exhibit myself, I still would not think of myself as an enslaved person. I looked straight back at that awful audience and despised them. I stayed silent, but inside, I screamed, "I hate you all!"

Is that when you spotted Samuel Baker in the crowd of buyers?

Recalling that long-ago moment, Florence gives a faint smile: "Yes, he was there to acquire supplies and personnel for his expeditions. My angry gaze settled on him, and he stared right back at me. Something changed instantly. It felt like I was speaking directly to him, conveying my fury and distress. Somehow, Sam understood, and we both felt the connection. This man with curly reddish-brown hair, wearing a tweed suit, knew precisely how I felt.

Florence, that must have been extraordinary.

"Yes, it was a special moment. When Sam saw me - truly saw me - his entire demeanour changed. It was a turning point when he suddenly raised his hand. To my shock, this man was bidding for me, though his interest differed greatly from the other buyers. He was a man of tremendous curiosity and, above all, compassion."

So, what happened next, Florence, because he didn't win the auction, did he?

"No, you're right; you've done your research. I was officially sold to the Pasha who ruled Viddin. When the auction ended, Sam told his companion to collect their coats, go into the street and hail a closed carriage. He said he'd be along directly as he had something to do first.

He summoned Ali, my protector, saying: "I require your services." Later, Samuel told me that he had stuffed a massive wad of money into Ali's sash, saying, "I would like you to bring that girl to me at the back of the house."

Indeed, that was risky for him, wasn't it, Florence?

Certainly, if anyone had discovered what Ali had done, my protector would have been executed. But Ali swore to me that no one would know it was him. I shall always be grateful for that precious assurance. Ali guided me to the gate and helped me up into the darkened carriage. He wished me well, and I replied, "May Allah reward you for your kind deed."

Florence! It's like an Arabian romance. Were you frightened and confused?

"As the carriage moved off, both my hands were shaking. I looked at Sam and thought, "He owns me," but his kind manner and obvious decency reassured me. But for the second time, I was a stolen woman."

I've read that you crossed the Danube together and joined Samuel

on his travels.

"Yes, Sam saw in me, not just a person to rescue. Initially, I was sceptical since all my experiences had made me wary of many things, including the intentions of strangers. But Sam was different; he treated me with a rare and refreshing kindness."

And how did your relationship develop from there?

"It evolved most unexpectedly. Samuel gave me a chance to escape my past life, and though it was filled with uncertainty, it was also full of hope. Our mutual respect and admiration turned into something more profound. We married in 1865, and from then on, we were partners in life and exploration."

What were your travels in Africa like? Can you describe them a little?

"Yes. Africa was both a paradise and a burden. We crossed vast landscapes, from the Nile to the continent's heart. I learned quickly how to navigate these wild places and understand the cultures and people we encountered. It was a world so different from everything I'd known. Yet, it became a part of me. Samuel and I grew close through these adventures, and they were the essence of our shared life."

Such unknowns must have been daunting. Florence, what was the most demanding part of your travels?

"Oh, there were so many complicated and trying moments — disease, hostile encounters with locals, the sheer physical strain of the difficult terrain. Perhaps the biggest test was earning the trust and respect of the local tribes and navigating the intricacies of their societies. Doing this was crucial for our survival and success and took a lot of patience and empathy."

Can you share any particularly demanding events during your time in Africa?

"Certainly. While exploring the Nile's source, we encountered hostile local groups, dangerous terrain, and much illness. In one place, a crisis could have ruined the entire expedition. A local tribal chief became hostile toward us and our crew. Tensions ran dangerously high, and violence seemed imminent.

I stayed calm but determined to deal with the issue. So, I engaged with the chief directly, showing him respect. I even used a few words in the local language that I had learned. This friendly approach transformed things, and we went on our way unharmed."

That story shows great courage. What else was a triumph in Africa?

"Perhaps one of the most memorable was our finding and naming Lake Albert, or Nyanza as it's called in several Bantu languages. Samuel wrote a popular book about this, explaining that he wanted to stick with his travels "as the insignificant worm slowly bores its way into the hardest oak.

I don't think one single achievement sums up all our travels. Being a pioneering explorer with Samuel and the friendships we made along the way certainly defied people's expectations. Together, we lived a life of adventure and purpose. I was delighted when Samuel was recalled to London to be knighted in 1872 by Queen Victoria for his explorations in Africa.

As a former Caucasian slave that Samuel had rescued and later married, our much-publicised union was regarded as scandalous. Sadly, her Majesty would not meet me since, on behalf of society, she frowned on premarital relationships and disliked our unconventional story."

Incredible, after all that you'd been through, how do you feel about that most royal snub?

"Let's just say that, at the time, it made me aware that in Queen Victoria's England, personal conduct and reputation were essential for anyone in the public eye. I was glad when, as husband and wife, we returned to Egypt and our pleasing home here in Cairo."

What a story! Thank you again, Florence, for sharing it with me.

"I'm glad our story continues to inspire and resonate with others." Opening a nearby drawer, Florence removes a slender book encased in rich, reddish-brown soft leather. "Please accept this small token of our pleasurable meeting today."

Printed on the first page is: "Account of the Discovery of the Second Great Lake of the Nile, Albert Nyanza", and boldly in the centre: Samuel White Baker, 1865.

Florence, this is such a lovely gift. It's been an honour to hear from you directly, and I will always treasure this book.

NOTE: After years of exploration, Cairo became a comfortable and familiar base for the Bakers. Its cosmopolitan nature connected them with other expatriates, and they engaged in the city's vibrant cultural life. When Samuel died in 1894, Florence remained in Egypt, dedicating her life to perpetuating her husband's achievements and memory.

Florence described the couple's adventures in her book The Life of Captain Sir Samuel Baker, detailing their African explorations. Through lectures and public speaking, she actively promoted Samuel Baker's legacy. She enthusiastically shared their story and emphasised his contributions to exploration.

For more about this remarkable woman, read Pat Shipman's colourful and excellent book The Stolen Woman, published by Bantam Press in 2004.

LOU VON SALOMÉ

1861–1937

Lou Von Salomé, a Russian-born psychoanalyst, philosopher, and writer, was known for her close relationships with Nietzsche, Freud, and the poet Rilke. She was a formidable intellectual who broke traditional gender roles, and her work in psychoanalysis and literature remains influential.

"The greatest thing in life is to learn to love and be loved in return."

Lou Andreas-Salomé: Her Life and Work by Rainer Maria Rilke

LOU VON SALOMÉ

I'm in Gottingen, Germany, in the mid-1930s to chat with the formidable and cerebral Lou von Salomé.

We're meeting in her private apartment, a welcoming space for friends and visitors where stimulating conversations about literature, philosophy, and the arts occur regularly. Long recognised as an intellectual giant, Lou is an almost magical source of inspiration to those fortunate enough to encounter her face-to-face. Few people meeting Salomé forget the experience.

Stepping into Salomé's study, I am immediately enveloped by the intellectual atmosphere. The room is packed with books and manuscripts. A sturdy wooden desk overflows with papers, notebooks and letters from various intellectuals and friends. Personal mementoes and photos lie scattered around, including framed pictures of Friedrich Nietzsche, Sigmund Freud, and Rainer Maria Rilke - all significant figures in her life.

After a short wait, Salomé enters. Now in her 70s, Lou refers to herself as a "little old woman," but meeting her today I encounter a dignified, elegant person with striking features. Lou wears her hair stylishly and looks young for her advanced years. She wears a long skirt, a blouse with a high collar, and a tailored jacket.

"It's so kind of you to come all this way to see me. I'm looking forward to our conversation. Where will we start?" she asks, fluent in English despite it not being her primary language."

Good evening, Von Salomé; it's an honour to speak with you. Like many others who admire your achievements, I find it fascinating that your life intersects with that of many other great thinkers. Please will you talk about your younger days and what led you to the impressive work you're known for?

"It's a complicated story, but I was born in St. Petersburg in 1861 to a Russian army general of French Huguenot descent and a Danish mother. For that particular time, my upbringing was unconventional. For example, my father strongly encouraged my intellectual pursuits. That was rare for a girl in the 19th century. His early stimulus provoked my lifelong passion for learning and philosophy."

Can we begin with one of the most complex parts for most people to understand: Nietzsche's work? I know that you sought him out. How did that finally happen?

"Please do call me Frau Lou or Salomé. Yes, I was enamoured with Friedrich Nietzche's work and pushed hard to meet him. We finally connected in 1882 through Paul Rée, a mutual friend, a distinguished author, physician, and philosopher."

You also made it your business to try to popularise his thinking, right?

"Correct. Nietzsche was drawn to my intellect and ideas. For those trying to understand Nietzsche, I interpreted his work as a profound exploration of individualism and the struggle against conventional morality. I explained his concept of the Übermensch as advocating for creating personal values and authenticity.

For the growing number of curious people interested in Nietzsche's philosophy, I described it as a response to existential despair. Nietzche urged people to embrace life's complexities and uncertainties with courage and creativity. He loved my interpretation and got so carried away that he kissed me and even proposed marriage!"

Well, marriage was off the agenda since you studiously avoided it, at least of the conventional kind, right?

"Correct, I've always cherished my freedom and independence. Despite his obvious attraction to me, my relationship with Nietzsche remained one of intellectual camaraderie rather than romantic involvement. This led me to adopt the idea of a triangle between him, Rée, and myself. It was one of many triangles I formed."

Salomé, this concept of a permanent triangle, sometimes involving sex, was highly controversial and, even much later, rarely spoken about. What led you to adopt such an unusual approach?

"It was less like a triangle and more like a mobile, with a delicate balance of interconnected parts. Each part represented a person, free to move and interact with the others, creating a dynamic and ever-changing relationship. I know it's controversial, but I chose this because of my desire for unrestrained intellectual and emotional freedom. But I admit it's not for the weak-hearted. It isn't enough to exist; one must attempt to live deeply and purposefully. In the realm of love as in thought, we must cast aside the chains of convention and explore the depths of our souls."

Well, you certainly did that, Frau Lou. Your radical views seriously clash with society's traditional notions, don't they?

"Absolutely! My long-lasting, purely formal marriage with Friedrich Carl Andreas lasted from 1902 until he died in 1930. We were married for 28 years, but the many triangles I created were unconventional. They upset some people, including my mother. My husband was a German orientalist and scholar, but we maintained separate lives and respected each other's need for independence.

My unusual relationship with Andreas allowed me to continue my work and relationships with other intellectuals without being confined by society's expectations. Let me put it this way: our marriage was a testament to the possibility of a loving and respectful relationship. It did not require the sacrifice of individual freedom."

Given your rejection of the conventional and your desire for independence, can you sum up your thoughts on the relationship between love and freedom?

"Ah, that's a good question. The perennial dance between love and freedom is a paradox that has always fascinated people. In its purest form, love is an expansive, even explosive force. It ought to liberate rather than confine. Yet, within the norms of society, love often becomes a binding contract. It is too much like a rope being tightened and restricting the very essence of individuality and freedom. In that situation, the true nature of love is severely tested."

Yes, and often found wanting. As I had hoped, Salomé, you have offered a deep perspective. It leads me to ask how this dynamic you've described plays out in other relationships.

"In general relationships, this dynamic shows up as a delicate balance. True intimacy requires a willingness to be vulnerable. Intertwining one's essence with another demands respect for the other's autonomy."

So, do you regard any relationship that stifles personal growth and freedom as inherently flawed?

"I do, yes. The most profound connections encourage each person to flourish independently while growing together. They encourage you to recognise another person's intrinsic value without the barrier of possessiveness or control."

Given the tensions you have mentioned, what guidance can you give people on navigating any relationship's inevitable ups and downs?

"Quite simply, conflict is unavoidable in any meaningful relationship. This is when the resilience and depth of the connection become tested. A relationship becomes fortified through this process, and each conflict becomes an opportunity for deeper understanding and connection."

Regarding relationships, Frau Lou, how did you come to work with the father of psychotherapy?

"I met Freud in Vienna much later in life, in 1911. By then, I was already a published author interested in psychoanalysis. Freud and I developed a solid professional relationship. I was among the first women to join his inner circle, the Vienna Psychoanalytic Society. Freud appreciated my contributions to psychoanalysis, particularly my insights into female sexuality and the psychology of love."

Salomé, there's a famous story that Freud despaired if you weren't sitting in the audience when he gave his lectures. Is that true?

"Ah, yes! Freud appreciated my presence at his lectures. He considered me both intellectually stimulating and a source of inspiration. Freud often noted how my contributions enriched the discussions, reflecting my understanding of human psychology and relationships. Our interactions highlighted a mutual respect and fascination with each other's work."

And it was not just Freud who felt like that, Salomé. You're renowned for impacting nearly all those who have met you. Some even accuse you of being a complete flirt!

"I suppose I have been a flirt, but less so now. It was my way of getting to know some of the people I valued at the time. It also encouraged many I met to be more creative and open with me in their chosen area of interest."

Your writings on love and sexuality are also far ahead of their time. Can you discuss these views and how your contemporaries have reacted to them?

"I see you've done your research. My work, especially 'The Erotic,' delved into the complexities of human desire and the psychological underpinnings of love. At that time, this was revolutionary and often met with resistance. However, Freud and some of my contemporaries appreciated my perspective. They thought it added a new dimension to psychoanalytic theory."

Another prominent figure in your earlier life was the poet Rainer Maria Rilke. This relationship with him was also both personal and professional. How did you influence his work?

"Rainer and I met in 1897 when he was starting his career. We shared a deep emotional and intellectual bond. I encouraged him to explore his inner world through poetry and face his fears and desires. This significantly influenced his work during our time together, including our travels to Russia. Rilke often said I helped him find his voice as a poet. Our relationship was one of mutual inspiration and growth."

Apart from your relationships with these significant people, your extensive literary work includes many best-selling novels. What do you see as highlights from your writing career?

"I've written novels, essays, and psychoanalytic works. My best sellers include Ruth, Fenitschka, and Looking Back, which is my autobiography, though people tell me it's not revealing enough!

As you'd expect, my writing often explores themes of individuality, freedom, and the intricate nature of human relationships. I have always sought to challenge society's norms and provoke thought through my writing."

Despite your significant contributions, like many talented women, your work has frequently been overshadowed by the men you associate with.

"It is certainly tough at times. I am often seen through the lens of my relationships with men like Nietzsche, Rée, and Freud rather than being recognised for my own work. However, I have never allowed these perceptions to deter me. I am driven by a passion for knowledge and an unwavering belief in the importance of my contributions. Over time, I have found that staying true to myself and my vision is the most effective way to navigate these challenges."

I understand. Looking back on your colourful, some would say exotic life, Frau Lou, what do you regard as your most significant achievement?

"That's hard to say, and I prefer to leave that to others. But I admit I am proud of my contributions to psychoanalysis and literature. These seem to have affected influential thinkers and writers. If I had to choose the most significant result, it would be living authentically and unapologetically and pursuing my passions and ideas despite the constraints."

Your life Frau Lou has influenced literature, psychoanalysis, and feminism. Can you look ahead and suggest how you expect women's roles to evolve?

"That's a topic close to my heart. I am glad to have witnessed the gradual awakening of women to their potential and the recognition of the value of their voices. In the past, women have often been relegated to the background, defined by their relationships with men. However, from my engagement with thinkers and artists, I always return to the importance of fully developing the self. If my life's journey has any value, it is perhaps to show what women can achieve when they unapologetically pursue their intellect and passions."

Yes, that is so important. To be much more specific, what are the most significant challenges women face today in achieving true equality?

"An enduring challenge I see is how society's expectations keep altering. As women, we still have to navigate the delicate balance between personal ambition and the roles society prescribes for us. Whatever the progress so far, there remains a pervasive tendency to judge women based on their choices in the personal and professional realms. True empowerment stems from the freedom to choose one's path, unencumbered by societal norms."

Indeed, navigating societal expectations must be difficult. Given your emphasis on intellectual freedom, how do you feel about the impact of technology on modern relationships?

"I'm no expert on technology but it has the potential to connect individuals across vast distances, allowing for intellectual exchanges that were once impossible. Yet, it can also create superficial interactions that lack depth. Right now, a handwritten letter can take weeks to reach its destination, fostering a certain depth in communication.

Yet faster methods, such as the telegraph and the telephone, are revolutionising long-distance communication. Then there are the new typewriters, changing how people write and produce documents. Electric light is also gaining widespread adoption, transforming homes, workplaces, and public spaces and altering social dynamics."

That's a most thoughtful perspective. You have often emphasised the importance of being authentic. Considering the complexity of relationships, the development of technology, and the challenges you have mentioned in society, how can we maintain authenticity?

"To remain authentic, one must cultivate a mindful relationship with technology. I am not entirely clear about this except to look for ways to avoid the constant noise and distractions from these new developments. Real human connections require presence through the written word or face-to-face interaction. Remember, true intimacy arises from vulnerability, honesty, and the willingness to share one's true self, regardless of the medium."

Your life is such an inspiration. Finally, I'd like to ask you what advice you would give young people who aspire to make their mark in the world of ideas.

"My advice is to remain curious and fearless in pursuing knowledge. Don't be afraid to challenge conventions and think independently.

Surround yourself with people who inspire and support you, but always stay true to your vision and passions."

Thank you, Frau Lou, for your shared wisdom. I've valued this time with you, and you have given me a lot to think about."

It's been a joy reflecting on these themes with you. Engaging with curious minds always invigorates my spirit and reaffirms the power of connection and dialogue.

NOTE: Few left Salomé's presence unaffected. Some, like Freud and the romantic poet Rilke, were transformed by interacting with her. It was equally incendiary when she finally achieved her much sought-after contact with the enigmatic philosopher Nietzsche. By explaining his philosophy to the broader world, Salomé created a lasting impact. From being a total non-entity, Nietzsche suddenly became an international celebrity. No wonder it turned his head, and he boasted, "I am dynamite."

To learn more about this remarkable woman and her story, you will enjoy Julia Vicker's book "Lou von Salomé" (McFarland & Company, 1950).

MARIA MONTESSORI

1870–1952

Maria Montessori, an Italian physician and educator, developed the Montessori method of education. Her revolutionary approach focused on child-led learning and respect for a child's natural development. It has influenced education systems worldwide and continues to affect educationalists.

"We give children the space to develop, grow, and choose.

The child is both the hope and the promise of mankind."

The Absorbent Mind, Montessori, 1949

MARIA MONTESSORI

I am in the heart of a city that holds a profound significance in the life of the remarkable educationalist Maria Montessori. On January 6, 1907, she launched the first Montessori school in Rome, the Casa dei Bambini. This event marked the beginning of her influential journey to world educational influence. The Italian city remains a pivotal location for her activities and the headquarters of the ever-growing Montessori movement.

I'll meet the famous educationalist in this meeting room shortly. Simple furnishings relax me, and I look forward to hearing her talk about her insights and experiences. Now in her eighties, she enters quietly. Her silver hair, neatly styled, frames her face, which carries the wisdom of decades spent pioneering education. She moves with a gentle purpose. Dressed in elegant, simple clothing, she exudes a friendliness that invites connection and shakes my hand in welcome. She also puts a small object on the table though without mentioning it.

Good day, Doctor Montessori. Your work has not only impacted countless lives but has also inspired a movement. Given your busy schedule, I'm delighted to have this conversation with you.

"Yes, today, in 1950, there are more than a thousand active Montessori schools, and more are on the horizon."

They confirm the enduring impact of your work.

"Thank you, it is certainly encouraging. Before the First World War, I worried that the earlier interest in my system was losing momentum. However, let me clarify that the Montessori method is not, as many think, a specific education method. It's a world philosophy applied to education anywhere. People now see it as a universal approach to teaching that is highly adaptable."

Could you share some insights from your early days influencing your journey?

"I'm happy to talk about my early life if you would like. I was born on August 31, 1870, in Chiaravalle, Italy. It's a small town near Ancona, where my father was a railroad worker. My mother, Renilde, came from a family of modest means but was very progressive in her thinking. She believed in firmly disciplining her children. That meant strict routines, such as schedules, from mealtimes to bedtime: these taught order, responsibility and respect for authority. A child who misbehaved would face corrective measures such as being sent to their room and denied privileges. I salute my mother for instilling these values, which have greatly influenced my journey."

How exactly did they affect you, Dr Montessori?

"In diverse ways. For example, as a youngster, I had a daily knitting quota to help low-income people. Next, I started looking for other things I could handle at home. For instance, whenever the tile floor needed cleaning, I assigned myself to wash a certain number of squares within a target time. I quite enjoyed it. Later, that experience helped me develop "exercises of practical life" for use in a Montessori school. All this took up a lot of energy, and when I was seriously ill, I recall telling my mother, "Do not worry, mother, I cannot die. I have too much to do."

At that time, education for girls was seldom encouraged. Still, my mother nurtured my early curiosity and intellectual development. At twelve, I wanted to become an engineer, and a year later, in 1883, I enrolled in classes at an all-boys technical school."

So, what happened to that engineering ambition?

"I had a change of heart. I can't explain where my new preference for medicine came from; it was more of a mystical experience. It happened all in a moment. Somehow, I knew instantly that I should study medicine, something no woman in Italy had ever done. My relatives, particularly my father, were shocked. However, he stopped short of forbidding it. I became the first woman to attend medical school in

Italy by enrolling at the Sapienza University of Rome medical school, studying physics, maths and natural sciences."

Pursuing a medical career in the late 19th century must have demanded enormous courage and determination. What were some of the obstacles you faced during your medical studies?

"You can't get more basic than being refused entry to medical school! Opposition came from all sorts of quarters. But I was determined to become a doctor. In those days, many prejudices existed against women becoming involved in medicine. I faced serious, depressing and sustained scepticism from professors and classmates. They doubted my capabilities because I was a woman. Yet despite them, I nurtured a deep-seated belief in my potential."

It must have been difficult, so how did you overcome all these obstacles?

To be allowed to attend medical school, I appealed to many authorities. I made a perfect nuisance of myself. I even wrote to Pope Leo, begging for his help. To the surprise of many people, Papa noticed and approved of my ambition. He issued one of his orders, saying it was all right for girls to be doctors. That and the support from my family, plus my perseverance, kept me going. When I graduated with honours in 1896, I became one of the first female doctors in Italy."

What a triumph. After becoming a physician, why did you move into the field of education, which eventually became your life's work?

"My education journey was partly due to luck. As a doctor in the early 1900s at a specialist Institute in Rome, I began working with children with developmental disabilities. Their progress opened my eyes to the potential of all children, regardless of their circumstances. I realised that traditional educational methods often failed."

Can you tell me more about that, Dr Montessori?

Traditional schools didn't fully engage the children, so I began developing new approaches based on my observations and understanding of child psychology. My learning eventually laid the groundwork for the Montessori Method.

Could you share a real-life example that helped develop your thinking and approach?

"Certainly. Let's see. Well, one particular child, a young boy named Bruno, made a profound impression on me. Due to his condition, they labelled Bruno as incapable of learning. However, through the carefully designed activities I developed, he began showing remarkable progress, and people took note."

Your experiences with Bruno must have been enriching.

"It was. The Bruno experience convinced me we must tailor education to each child's needs and abilities. It seemed wrong to force all children to conform to a one-size-fits-all approach. That realisation was a pivotal moment. It solidified my commitment to developing a new educational paradigm."

What happened next?

"My focus shifted to mainstream education. My previous work with children suffering from disabilities had laid the foundation. I now realised that the principles I had developed could benefit all children. The Montessori Method evolved through a process of continuous refinement and observation.

I created a carefully prepared environment where children could learn independently and at their own pace, using specialised materials that encouraged hands-on learning. This approach respected each child's learning journey and encouraged self-direction and exploration."

Your method emphasises the importance of the environment in education. Could you also describe how you developed the materials

used in Montessori classrooms?

"Yes. It's a meticulous approach. I design materials to be sensory and tactile. These help children engage with abstract ideas by having concrete experiences. For instance, materials like the Pink Tower and the Painted Tablets help children sharpen their sensory perceptions and understand concepts like size, shape, and colour."

Can you explain these two materials and their role in your approach?

"Certainly. These two are essential to support children's sensory development. They help with visual discrimination of size and colour. The Pink Tower is one of our most recognisable materials, designed to help young children develop their understanding of dimension and order. It consists of ten wooden cubes of different sizes.

Children learn to recognise differences in size as they manipulate the cubes, from the smallest to the largest. Handling and placing the cubes in a specific order develops hand-eye coordination and agility. It also indirectly introduces the decimal system, as the cubes increase in size by increments of one cubic centimetre."

And what about the Colour Tablets, how do they work?

"Our Colour Tablets focus on the visual senses - specifically colour perception and differentiation. The materials invite children to explore abstract concepts through hands-on manipulation, leading to a deeper understanding of their environment. Through indirect and enjoyable learning experiences, these tools also prepare children for future academic subjects like mathematics, art, and geometry.

Dr. Montessori, can you share some moments or challenges that affected your development as an educator?

"My journey has involved many challenges. For instance, I faced opposition from the start to gaining recognition and support for my methods. My ideas often met with resistance from traditional educators and institutions."

What other obstacles did you face?

One particular personal challenge that greatly influenced my life and work was my relationship with Giuseppe Montesano, a fellow physician. Our son Mario was born in 1898, and by choice, I never married, which was unusual and socially frowned upon. There was then a great emphasis on traditional family structures and values. My status as a single mother proved troublesome. As an independent and assertive woman, this sometimes clashed with the expectations of men around me."

Did that include your father? Did he find it hard to accept a non-traditional approach to your personal and professional life?

"He was a traditionalist, but I would prefer not to discuss that now. However, my decision to remain single and focus on my professional work while raising Mario reflected my commitment to educational philosophy. However, balancing my professional life with my home responsibilities was difficult.

Did that commitment come under severe strain, or was it just a case of navigating the pressures?

"You make it sound easy! One extremely stressful time was when I was deeply engrossed in my work, and Mario fell ill. Maintaining his care while pursuing my professional responsibilities proved exceptionally demanding. However, the experience reinforced my understanding of the importance of nurturing the whole child - emotional, physical, and intellectual."

You've travelled extensively promoting the Montessori Method. When you arrived in America in 1913, you were one of the most famous women in the world. How did these travels influence your perspective on education and your approach to teaching?

"My travels have broadened my perspective. Visiting different countries and observing diverse educational systems made me see the universality and adaptability of the Montessori Method. People often don't realise that each culture and educational setting presents unique challenges and opportunities.

For instance, in India and the United States, I learned how the Montessori approach could be arranged to fit differing cultural contexts while maintaining the Montessori core principles. Such understanding reinforced my belief in the method's flexibility and potential to benefit children everywhere."

Nevertheless, your approach upset respected education experts like William Kilpatrick. He viewed your method negatively and actively campaigned against it.

"Yes, you are well informed. We disagreed fairly fundamentally. However, many who had accepted Kilpatrick's negative views about my methods later changed their minds. The growth of my approach continues to attract supporters. My focus on early learning gradually came into its own, along with self-motivation and well-designed instructional materials."

Your approach to education still attracts criticism, for example, that it's expensive. What do you say to such views?

"When someone complains education is expensive, I love the reply: 'Have you tried the cost of ignorance?' I understand the concerns, but sound education is seldom cheap. My approach keeps evolving, and I believe it will continue."

Dr Montessori, what achievements make you feel most proud when you reflect on your life and career?

"Most proud? I am most satisfied that the Montessori Method has profoundly impacted education worldwide. Seeing children thrive and develop a love for learning through this approach is gratifying. The worldwide adoption of Montessori schools and training programs shows the method's enduring relevance. It's a great source of fulfilment to me that my work has influenced educational practices. I am happy that it has contributed to the well-being and development of so many children across the globe."

Looking back, is there anything you would have done differently or any advice you would offer educators today?

"I encourage educators to remain open-minded and flexible. To them, I say: keep considering the needs and individuality of each child. The core principles of the Montessori Method — respect for the child, the importance of a prepared environment, and the value of hands-on learning — remain timeless. My advice to educators today would be to embrace these principles while also adapting to the evolving needs of the children and the educational landscape."

Dr. Montessori, it has been a privilege to hear about your experiences and insights directly from you.

"Thank you for the opportunity to reflect on my journey. It's been a pleasure sharing my experiences and thoughts." Montessori hands me the small object she had put on the table when she arrived for our conversation. "This wooden puzzle is to remember our unusual talk."

That's so unexpected and kind of you. Please tell me what this puzzle represents for you.

"It's used in our schools and confirms my belief in hands-on learning and independence. It'll remind you of the importance of exploration, curiosity, and the power of discovery and learning through play and problem-solving. I hope you enjoy it."

NOTE: Between 1950 and 2024, Montessori schools grew from about 1,000 to a staggering 30,000, and they are in 130 countries worldwide. To the present day, the Montessori method continues to impact education worldwide profoundly. Studies and reports over the years have consistently shown that Montessori students often outperform their peers in traditional schools in areas such as literacy, maths, and social skills. These students display higher independence, creativity, and problem-solving abilities.

Some critics argue that the Montessori approach may not suit all children, particularly those who require more structure or direct instruction. Despite her critics, Dr Montessori was nominated for the Nobel Prize three times.

For more insight into this remarkable physician, feminist, social reformer and educator, an excellent biography is Maria Montessori by Rita Kramer, Basic Blackwell, 1976

COLETTE

1873–1954

Colette, a French novelist, actress, and journalist, is a literary figure of immense significance. Her vivid and sensual writing, best seen in her novel Gigi, defied societal norms and established her as one of France's most respected literary figures. Her exploration of womanhood, sexuality, and independence in her writing significantly influenced feminist literature, enlightening a generation of readers. Her other notable works, including Chéri, The Vagabond, and The Pure and the Impure, further cement her literary legacy.

"When she raises her eyelids, it's as if she were taking off all her clothes."

Colette, Claudine and Annie, 1903

COLETTE

In a modest Paris café, I am to meet Colette, the French literary genius who has left an indelible mark on the world of literature. Now in her mid-60s, she lives in a 9 Rue de Beaujolais apartment, a short walk from this café, overlooking the superb gardens of the Palais-Royal. Colette moved here in 1938. Now, with arthritis causing increasing mobility problems, she has said it is probably her final retreat.

Despite her mobility issues, Colette's resilience and determination inspire countless others. Her Parisian sanctuary, far from being a writer's hideaway, is a vibrant hub for visitors and friends.

I have been told that those who encounter Colette sometimes find her bold demeanour somewhat distancing. Her lifelong dedication to her craft and independence can be mistakenly interpreted as aloofness. It explains why I'm approaching our conversation with slight wariness.

On entering the café, I soon spot the celebrated author seated at a table. We exchange smiles, and she gestures for me to sit, but there's no handshake. Colette's hair, once wild and untamed like a coiled serpent reaching her knees, is now reduced to whipped cream with flashes of silver amongst the blue-grey. Discreetly observing the woman opposite me, I am utterly captivated by her enduring beauty and compelling presence. Once I am settled, she is the first to speak.

"Well, It's good to get out like this as I seldom feel like making the effort these days. Thank you for suggesting we meet here. How shall we start?"

This warm-hearted welcome puts me at ease, and to my relief, she seems less intimidating than expected.

Madame Colette, can we begin with your early childhood and how it affected you and your approach to writing?

"Just call me Colette, please! That's as good a place to start as any. Let me see. Well, first, I was born Sidonie-Gabrielle Colette in 1873 in the small village of Saint-Sauveur-en-Puisaye in Burgundy, France. My father was a tax collector, and my mother, Sido, was a homemaker. How's that for our beginning?"

Perfect. In your autobiographical essays about your life with your mother, Colette, you vividly portray her strong character. For example, you often mention her love of nature and how it influenced your writing.

"Entirely true. My mother and her beloved countryside deeply affected my literary voice. She was progressive, what one might call a free spirit, and she was an independent thinker.

Can you suggest anything especially memorable?

"Well, for instance, she expected me to be able to read by the time I was three! More importantly, she encouraged me to explore the natural world and develop my opinions as I grew. Sido approached the issue of child development by constantly rejecting society's expectations and limitations. Her way of life helped cultivate a curious mind, stimulating me to appreciate life's sensual and natural themes. These became central to my writing.

Sido also thought formal schooling was rather pointless. Still, she ensured I was well-read and encouraged me to engage in intellectual discussions. Her love for books and storytelling was infectious, nurturing my passion for literature. Through it, I gained the confidence to be a writer."

That was a precious asset. Yet you also wrote how, in many ways, you had lost your childhood.

"That's true. While I adored Sido, it was a strict upbringing. She was highly demanding and continued that way all her life and was quite possessive. For instance, when I began feeling more independent, I cut off my incredibly long and demanding hair that my mother used to brush every day until it shone. Learning of this outrage, she protested: "*You have disposed of a precious trust I confided to you.*"

Once I was a full adult, though, we were a lot apart. While staying with my first husband's family, I played happily with the many children there. I came to appreciate what I had been missing with Sido. Somehow, those new fruitful interactions recovered some of my lost childhood. I was astonished at the difference between their family life and mine."

You put it well in your book My Apprenticeships. You complained of being broken to an outward show of obedience. So you rebelled inwardly and eventually outwardly.

"Exactly, and that rebellion fuelled an unstoppable desire to write."

Was there any specific moment when the urge to write began to take over your life?

"That's an easy one. I went to Paris with my father in 1889 and visited Monsieur Willy. He was a well-known writer and publisher aged 30, and I was just 16. Willy encouraged me to write. He was erudite, forceful, and playful. He was always making puns and teasing me. When I returned from Paris, I was madly in love with him. We began a secret correspondence. I sent my love letters on distinguished-looking grey-blue paper since this seemed worthy of my feelings. Then, much to the distress of his family and despite our age difference, I married him when I was 20.

His family wrote me off as a libertine and a fortune hunter. As you may know, Willy was the libertine and didn't even possess a fortune, eventually dying in poverty. I initially refused to believe Willy was an absolute roué. But I was quickly disillusioned when, almost immediately after our wedding, I discovered that he was being unfaithful to me. I was devastated and went into a deep depression, and it took a long time to recover."

Even so, you settled down and started writing seriously. How do you now regard that time?

"Looking back, the only word I can find is "frustrating. I wrote under his name for years because I was unknown, and my work sold better that way. At least it allowed me to hone my craft without the pressure of public scrutiny."

What was it like writing under Willy's name, apart from being frustrating?

"A mixed experience, partly liberating since I could experiment and find my voice. Inevitably, though, without recognition, it became stifling. This failure made me determined to succeed independently."

Is it true that Willy locked you in a room until you wrote what he wanted?

"Yes, it's true. However, I probably could have escaped if I'd been determined to do so. After more than a decade toiling away at interminable articles, books, and commentary, I finally began rebelling against publishing under his name and being part of Willy's infamous "factory" of writers."

While in the factory, you produced the notorious Claudine series based on much of your early life. How did that come about?"

"Typical of Willy, he dismissed my first attempts to write a novel, telling me they were juvenile. He took them and shoved them in a drawer. One day, three years after I had first written the entire Claudine series, money was tighter than usual. Willy scrabbled about in numerous drawers for something to sell and dug out my first Claudine manuscript. After quickly scanning it and the other books, I heard him mutter: "I'm a complete fool".

Belatedly, he realised they had commercial potential because of their racy, some say indecent content. He immediately rushed off, but not before urging me to add yet more spicy content. He instantly arranged the publication of the first in the series: Claudine at School. Initially, it was a slow burner, which was disappointing. But it became a literary sensation when Willy called in some favours to get it reviewed. Of course, for the rest of the series, which sold in thousands, Willy went crazy. He peddled endless Claudine-linked wares such as jewellery, pins, necklaces, ink, pens, notebooks, and other awful dross. "

Your Claudine novels from 1900 to 1903 were hugely popular, but the public attributed their success to Willy, didn't they?

"It's true. Much to my fury, my authorship remained a secret, and I failed to receive the recognition I deserved. Meanwhile, our marriage was not going well, and in 1906, we separated."

Leaving you to fend for yourself both financially and professionally?

"Yes, you are correct! I turned to the stage—not just because I wanted to perform, which I did, but to support myself. I built a public identity separate from Willy and his influence."

You also invested considerable time preparing for this new life by studying mime, exercising with a trainer, and regularly using a wooden bar. Looking back, Colette, on that time, are there any particular moments you strongly recall as important?

"Well, I loved pushing the boundaries of what was considered acceptable. I still cherish the memory of my most disreputable performances at the Moulin Rouge in 1907 when I acted in Rêve d'Égypte or Dream of Egypt. As a mummy brought to life, I did a highly suggestive dance with my fellow performer, Mathilde de Morny, known as Missy. Our performance ended with us having a lengthy kiss, which scandalised Parisian society and the police intervened over its apparent indecency."

Can you tell me more about your involvement with Missy?

Ah, Missy. She was nobility yet defied it at every turn. Here was a woman unlike any I'd ever encountered: elegant, aristocratic, yet utterly fearless. She lived as herself, happily wearing trousers and a man's coat. It was scandalous for the time. I'd never seen such strength, such defiance. Wc made quite the pair. We lived together openly for a while, thumbing our noses at convention. It was a rare freedom and love in the face of a world that demanded women like us stay invisible.

But freedom can prove to be complicated, can't it, Colette?

"You're so right. By 1912, the fierce love we shared was wearing thin. Missy loved me and supported my writing, whims, and everything, but I began to feel confined, even in her embrace. Once more, I found myself drawn to men.

Since you had been so happy in your relationship with Missy, what exactly went wrong?

"I'm not entirely sure. Perhaps it was curiosity. Or maybe it was that familiar pull of the unknown. Missy sensed it, but the ending wasn't marked by fights or slammed doors. Instead, there was a gentle drifting away, yet we both knew. That summer, we parted.

Missy left a hole in my life but gave me something that remained: courage. She'd taught me to love without apology, to write without flinching. After our life together, I felt brave, and without shame, I wrote about love and identity as I knew it. Missy still lingers in my words, art, and refusal to bend to society. She'd been a companion, a lover, and, in many ways, the key to the woman I was becoming. Missy is woven into every step of my journey, and I am forever grateful for that."

You reportedly even wore a collar with a tag reading "I belong to Missy" as a symbolic gesture of devotion to this partner.

"I see no reason to deny it. That label acknowledged our relationship.

Yes, it was daring, but more importantly, she was a great source of inspiration. Our times together were some of the happiest periods of my life. My lovers have always been my muses, helping me explore different aspects of my identity and creativity."

Can you tell me about the immediate time after Missy?

"My time on the stage let me express a different side of my creativity, which was more physical and immediate than my writing. I was also breaking new ground as a woman in a male-dominated world of both literature and theatre. I never apologised for my choices. Most controversially, I embraced my bisexuality, defying conventional gender norms through my performances and personal life."

Your stage work included some bold and scandalous performances, such as bearing a breast, as well as that prolonged lesbian kiss! Do you regret that now?

"Of course not. They helped establish me as a public figure. I also reclaimed my literary work and continued writing under my own name. One of my earliest roles was acting in Claudine à Paris, a play based on my novel. This intrigued the public and allowed me to take advantage of the popularity of my Claudine series, which had already captivated readers with its semi-autobiographical tale of a young woman's life in France."

You didn't stop there, did you?

"Certainly not; I quickly moved beyond merely adapting my written work for the stage. I plunged into all aspects of theatrical production, from acting to dancing and writing scripts. I wrote more novels, essays, and stories and steadily acquired the acclaim that had eluded me during our marriage."

In summary, Colette, what did this creative stage time do for you?

"Sum it all up? Well, it was a great time for personal growth. I learned to navigate the world on my terms, becoming more assertive and independent. That also showed up in my later writing. By the time I left the stage to focus once more on writing, I'd become recognised and respected in both the literary and theatrical worlds. But it wasn't until I was 37 that my first novel, La Vagabonde, was published with my name actually on the cover. It tells the story of divorced woman Renée Néré, who becomes a dancer in music halls to support herself."

Was it unashamedly based on your own stage experiences? How did seeing your name on the book cover make you feel at the time?

"Certainly, the book reflected my time on the stage. And seeing that single word, Colette, on the front of my book was so liberating...at last, I felt seen."

Talking of liberation, your experience of love heavily influences your writing.

"It's true that I had a few lovers...

Catching my quizzical look, Colette chuckles, adding, "...well, all right then, there were lots of lovers, both men and women. Each brought something different to my life and my work. As I once told a close friend: always take advantage of temptation that passes and indulge it."

Can you talk about other ways these many relationships have shaped your writing?

"Relationships, as you know, are a big part of my writing. They have given me a deeper understanding of love, desire, and human nature. My best work has come from a place of emotional truth, and my lovers helped me access that. Writing about my relationships has also allowed me to process my feelings and make sense of my experiences. It became a duty to write."

Can we now consider more of your challenges as a woman writer?

"So many challenges. The literary world remains male-dominated, and it's hard to be taken seriously as a woman writer. I've had to fight for my place and repeatedly prove myself. There's pressure to conform to society's expectations of what a woman should be. But I've always refused to be boxed in. I've written about women's lives and experiences, trying to be honest and unapologetic. I think that's why my work resonates with so many people. Living authentically, though, has brought constant disapproval from critics."

Why do you think such reactions persist?

"Because critics have always found my independence and outspokenness threatening. Even now, there's nearly always a significant backlash whenever I'm recognised with literary awards and accolades. Many people detest the idea of celebrating a woman who has so brazenly flouted social norms.

Though my work is widely read, some people dismiss it as trivial or immoral. That's mainly because it's penned by a woman who refuses to adhere to the traditional expectations of femininity. The objections are about my writing and what I represent - a woman who has dared to live and write on her terms."

Considering your experiences as a woman writer, how do you reconcile your individualistic approach with the collective efforts of those fighting for women's rights?

"What exactly do you mean?"

Well, there's the famous Nietzsche comment about groups of females who pursue women's rights as "deserving the whip and the harem." Did you ever support such an extreme view?

"No. What I rejected was a one-dimensional view of women's rights. I found such an approach naive, misguided, and counterproductive. A woman's strength and agency are best expressed through autonomy and sensuality, not organised political movements."

So, do you regard collective feminist efforts with scepticism or even contempt?

"Not contempt; it's more that I prefer women to celebrate their individualism and personal freedom."

Given your experiences and what you've had to put up with in rejection, Colette, what advice would you give aspiring writers?

"People always write to me seeking my advice on how they should proceed as a writer. I find these constant requests tiresome. All I can tell them is to write from your heart and don't fear being vulnerable. People find it hard to believe their unique perspective is their most important asset, so embrace it. And, of course, don't let anyone tell you that you can't do it. If you have a story to tell… tell it. The world needs more voices, especially those marginalised or previously silenced."

Our conversation naturally winds down. Colette and I slowly walk towards her apartment, mindful of her mobility challenges. I thank her profusely for our time together. To my utter enchantment, Colette bestows on me one of her famous sphynx-like smiles and gives me a generous parting hug. No wonder that countless people have fallen under her spell through the years. Colette's story vividly demonstrates the power of perseverance and the importance of staying true to oneself.

NOTE: In 1936, wearing sandals with lacquered brilliant red toenails, Colette was accepted into the exclusive French Academy of Literature. Rumours that she was being considered for a Nobel prize came to nothing, but if anyone deserved that elusive award, it was Colette.

Despite the challenges of arthritis, Colette remained intellectually sharp and creatively active. She refused to take painkillers because "they colour my mind."

She never knew how to stop writing, and her final book, *The Blue Lantern*, describes the experience of being increasingly immobilised in exquisite and heart-rending detail.

Colette died in her bed on 3rd August 1954, receiving the first state funeral for a French woman of letters reflecting the high esteem in which she was held. She remains an enduring symbol of the struggle for women's autonomy and the right to define themselves on their own terms. Her contributions to literature and her courage in living authentically have left an indelible mark. There is good reason why this woman is regarded in France and elsewhere as a national treasure.

For a gripping and complete account of Colette's life, go to the well-researched biography by Judith Thurman, Secrets of the Flesh, Bloomsbury Publishing, 2000.

For a more intimate approach following in the footsteps of Colette, don't miss the beautifully illustrated Colette's France-her Lives, her Loves, by Jane Gilmour, Hardie Grant Books, 2013.

MARIE STOPES

1880–1958

Marie Stopes was a British author, scientist, and pioneering advocate for birth control and women's reproductive rights. Her book Married Love in 1918 transformed societal views on sexuality. She founded the first birth control clinic in the UK, revolutionising women's access to contraception.

"A modern and humane civilisation must control conception or sink into barbaric cruelty to individuals."

Stopes, Married Love, 1918

MARIE STOPES

The discreet brass plaque on the front door says it all: Maternity, hygiene and birth control. Inside this famous, some say notorious, education and birth control clinic, there's a calm and welcoming atmosphere. Though modest, the waiting room, with simple wooden chairs, well-worn tables, and soft lighting, is clean and inviting. Pamphlets covering family planning, contraception, and reproductive health lie neatly stacked on a small table. Vibrant posters on the walls have messages such as "Your Body, Your Choices" and "Empower yourself with knowledge." The atmosphere is reassuring and almost homely, creating a sense of comfort and reassurance.

I will shortly meet the female dynamo who runs this and others nationwide. A nurse leads me upstairs to meet Marie Stopes in her office. She's impeccably dressed in a tailored skirt and blouse. Her demeanour is warm, yet you can tell she's a woman used to being in charge. She greets me with a brisk handshake, radiating energy and a sense of urgency. She must have many things on her mind, yet she seems fully alert and present for our conversation.

Thank you for agreeing to see me, Marie Stopes. I have many questions. Can we start with something that puzzles me, please?

"I'm happy to help with that. Please be seated. Just to let you know that I am due to give a talk in about half an hour. I trust we can get through by then. What exactly is puzzling you?"

My first question may surprise you. It's not about sex, clinics or avoiding abortions; it's about palaeontology."

"You're well-informed. So, you probably know that I graduated with a first-class degree in Botany from University College London. From there, I was awarded a fellowship at the University of Munich, where I researched botany and palaeobotany. I was also the youngest person to receive a Doctor of Science degree and the first female academic staff member in the science faculty of UCL."

Even in those early days, you already had a well-deserved reputation for intense concentration on work and leadership. Is there any specific project you're most proud of from that period of your life?

"Well, it sounds exotic, but I headed an expedition through the northern jungle of Japan, leading a party of thirty-nine men in my quest to find fossils."

A lone young white woman traveller in Japan at that time must have fascinated everyone you encountered.

"True, crowds of people often gathered. When I went to bathe, women and children were amazed at my white skin and wondered why I wore a "dress" to enter the water. The work was tiring, but the scenery lifted my spirits. I always decided where we would make camp, and despite the difficulties, I dared not show fear, which kept me going. We were rewarded by the fossils we discovered, which were the best we had obtained."

This leads me to ask what happened to the committed scientist, explorer, and academic who wrote Ancient Plants, which became a foundation text in palaeobotany.

"Yes, it's true I was a committed and trained academic. In 1911, I married Reginal Gates, a Canadian botanist. At the time, I thought we had a lot in common. Yet, it quickly emerged that we had difficulties regarding intimacy and sexual relations. For example, at first, I couldn't understand why I wasn't getting pregnant."

Is it true you were brought up to believe you had suddenly appeared out of nowhere?

"Perfectly true, yes. I then entered a marriage almost wholly ignorant of the essential facts of life. In my home with my parents, human sex was taboo, never spoken of at all."

And is it true that five years after you were married, you were still a

virgin?

"More unexpected questions! Yes, for the first year, I had no clue that my marriage was unusual. I had achieved married status, widely considered a woman's ultimate goal, and maintained my independence, which I deeply cherished. In desperation, I resorted to my training as an academic and ended up in the British Library researching about the female body."

And what did you learn from your reading there?

I finally learnt what it means to consummate a marriage. First, I learned much about the human body, the physiology of reproduction, the law, and, just as important, my rights, or lack of them, as a wife. I read pretty nearly every book in English, French, and German that was available on sex. I even wrote a play called Vectia about the whole issue. The trouble is that the Lord Chancellor got cold feet about it and refused a performing licence. Second, not long after that, I started writing my eventual bestseller, Married Love.

Regardless of Vectia's fate, you knew what you were getting into, didn't you?

"I appreciate the trouble you have taken to come prepared. It's always good to talk to someone well-informed. As a result of my experience, or rather lack of it, I wanted to end the dreadful ignorance suffered by so many others. I concluded that it was vital to explain to people, especially women, about sex, love and family planning. However, I went further and argued for birth control to improve women's health and mental happiness. Women have been kept in the dark for far too long. What we're doing here is not just medical work — it's revolutionary."

Another thing you got into was a new marriage. What difference did this make in the preparations for married love?

"Yes, I married my beloved Humphrey Roe just after publishing Married Love. We decided on a secret wedding and went to Lands End for our Honeymoon. His wisdom and support have made a big difference to me, and we are inseparable. Later, Humphrey helped run my first clinic and the Society for Constructive Birth Control, which I helped start in 1921."

You once told a friend, "I am writing a book that will electrify England." And it did! Your book Married Love sold an incredible million or more copies and was translated into 13 languages.

"Correct. I was inundated with thousands of letters from new readers and others seeking my advice. That, and my much-publicised legal action against my first husband for the non-consummation of the marriage, created what can only be described as a societal explosion. What happened was transformative and shifted society's collective thinking."

Your best-selling sex manual catapulted you into the public eye.

"It certainly did. It gave me a broader platform in 1918 to reach far more people. As I had anticipated, the book upset the medical and religious establishment. Many saw me as lewd and evil. They demanded my book be banned on the grounds of immorality."

The book ban never happened. Instead, sales went through the roof, with two thousand women buying my book in the first two weeks of publication. They wanted to know more about their bodies, about orgasms, and how to have a happy marriage. The books were circulated on factory floors, in soldiers' barracks, among friends and in lots of informal ways that confirmed its central importance in providing sex education.

Your radical publication arrived just when open discussions about sexuality were often unthinkable and shrouded in misinformation.

"Yes, it addressed the importance of sexual fulfilment within marriage and provided practical advice on sexual intimacy. I aimed to empower women by educating them about their bodies and rights within a marital relationship. Many people praised its candidness. Others hated it for being too explicit. Most importantly, it sparked conversations about sexual health that, as you say, were previously avoided in public discourse."

Did that sudden success spur you on to write more?

"Yes, it certainly did. A couple of years after Married Love, I published Wise Parenthood, which was a practical guide on birth control methods. That, too, sold extremely well. Also, my low-cost pamphlet, A Letter to Working Mothers, was deliberately written in a style my audience might feel comfortable with. This was advice to women on the importance of avoiding abortions. I explained why this illegal solution puts women in great physical danger."

Was that your final farewell to palaeontology?

"Absolutely. My publishing success had drawn me inexorably into sex education and beyond. A year after Wise Parenthood, I opened the first birth control clinic in Britain, along with Humphrey Vernon Rowe, who I later married. The clinics provide women with contraceptive information and, just as important, offer access to contraceptive devices."

You not only established contraceptive clinics, Marie, you even pioneered an inexpensive contraceptive device.

"True, I researched contraception with the same intensity I had once spent on palaeontology. My Prorace Cervical Cap is simple and easy to understand and requires internal fitting, which we do at our clinics. We mainly give it away or make a small charge to cover the cost.

Unfortunately, its success has become a problem. Many charlatans and companies have started selling cheap and low-quality imitations. They have even used my name to make these shameful products appear legitimate. Many are poorly fitted and fail in use. Frankly, it's an uphill struggle to persuade people, especially the poorest, to adopt the high-quality, low-cost versions we've developed."

At the same time, you turned yourself into a one-woman publishing factory, producing hundreds of books, papers and pamphlets. What was your next big production?

"After considerable research, I launched a 400-page textbook called Contraception. It was mainly aimed at the medical establishment."

Who naturally lapped it up? Right?

"Um, not exactly. What a terrible battle I've faced with it! The medical establishment hated me talking about medical things, as I wasn't medically trained. My PhD didn't impress them. Still, hundreds of doctors who bought the book wrote to congratulate me and thanked me for helping them understand what for many of them had been a mystery."

Another puzzle to unravel for me, Marie, is how you find time to produce so much. You've even published Love Songs for Young Lovers, a collection of poems that realised your literary talents and expanded your advocacy for love and marital harmony.

"Yes, I've felt driven to write about the whole sex subject to counter the incredible ignorance surrounding me. My early academic training and way of working efficiently helped hone my research and writing skills. So, I'm used to distilling complex scientific ideas into accessible formats for scholarly and general audiences. And while it's kind of you to give me the title of a one-woman publishing factory, I am not alone.

I tap into the creative potential of scores of assistants, nurses, and supporters who help me manage the day-to-day operations of our clinics. This support allows me to focus on writing and advocacy. My husband has also greatly supported me in setting up the clinics and helping with administrative tasks."

You seem to have mastered presenting your ideas to a broad audience.

"I'm still often labelled "scandalous" or "dangerous". But what's important is that we're building a future here where women are free to choose what they do with their bodies. I have used every means possible to counter the negative impression given by the medical and religious establishments. I even wrote a song, "Love in Danger", designed to raise awareness about the importance of birth control."

To my utter delight, Marie Stopes quietly begins to sing in a throaty but clear voice, at which two nurses quietly enter and join in the impromptu concert:

"My loved one and I, with a child at my breast,

We're contented and happy we lived with the best,

But alas for my love, he is now full of care,

For his health and his strength, they are almost spent,

And the burden of love is more than he meant."

One nurse whispers something in Marie Stopes' ear, at which she nods vigorously and stands up.

"I hope you enjoyed our impromptu concert. I'm afraid our time together has run out. I'm due to give a talk now. I also hope you enjoyed our conversation. Please feel free to take a copy of any of the pamphlets on display and pass them on to any friends who might find them useful.

I most certainly will. And thank you for the delightful song. I will

treasure the memory.

NOTE: The spread of Stopes' birth control advocacy has influenced reproductive rights movements worldwide. She helped empower women to have more control over their lives, contributing to smaller family sizes, improved maternal health, and greater gender equality. Not everyone was convinced, though, as this nursery rhyme suggests:

Jeanie, Jeanie, full of hopes,

Read a book by Marie Stopes,

But, to judge from her condition,

She must have read the wrong edition.

Also, Stope's unfortunate promotion of eugenics has dented her influence. However, the bigger picture is that her work in promoting contraception has had a profound and lasting impact on women's health and society.

Such was the extent of her written output that a three-ton lorry was required to transport all her papers bequeathed to the British Museum from her home in Surrey. It also took the museum staff some 18 years to complete a preliminary sorting of the vast range of material.

Two well-rounded books about Stopes include:

Marie Stopes, Ruth Hall, Andre Deutsch, 1977

Marie Stopes and the sexual revolution, by June Rose, Faber and Faber, 1992

An interesting talk on Stopes, her writings and their impact before World War 2 by Dr Claire Jones, University of Kent, is at: https://tinyurl.com/5yn57upy

COCO CHANEL

1883–1971

A French fashion designer, Chanel was a revolutionary force in the early 20th century, transforming women's fashion. She introduced the concept of casual elegance, liberating women from the constraints of corsets and crazy hair accessories. Her legacy includes the iconic Chanel No. 5 perfume and the enduring brand that bears her name.

"A girl should be two things: classy and fabulous."

Chanel: A Woman of Her Own by Axel Madsen, 1980

COCO CHANEL

Madame Chanel, now in her late seventies in 1959, graciously hosts our meeting above her legendary boutique at 31 Rue Cambon in Paris. This address is a cornerstone of Chanel's fashion empire in the heart of Paris's trendy 1st Arrondissement. It is a frequent meeting place for high-profile clients and collaborators. The top floor of the building also houses her private apartment, where we are to meet.

The epitome of the icon she has become, Madam Chanel, sits regally on a Louis XV sofa upholstered in gold brocade. Her impeccable black suit suggests the sharpness of a blade. In a long holder, she elegantly puffs one of her signature cigarettes, the smoke fusing with the lingering scent of Chanel No. 5. Her silver hair, styled in loose waves, embodies the effortless chic for which she is renowned. Chanel watches me closely as I sit across from her. She has a naturally commanding aura, yet her cordiality hints that our conversation will be more than a mere interview.

Madame Chanel, I can't help commenting on your apartment. Its décor perfectly fits how people see you. This elegant mixture of Eastern and Western influences, intricate lacquered screens, gilded mirrors, and crystal chandeliers all say 'Coco Chanel.'

She offers an appreciative smile, blowing a puff of smoke: "It is kind of you to say that. Please call me Coco. This place is indeed my sanctuary. I designed it as I do my clothes. Everything is in the details to achieve a balance between comfort and elegance. One must never forget comfort. It is not a luxury to be uncomfortable."

She gestures toward an ornate Coromandel screen. "Every piece here means something to me. I collect beauty, but it has to speak to me. I don't keep anything I don't love."

You are known to value simplicity, and your name is synonymous with understated elegance.

Her lips tighten: "I have spent my life cutting away what I find unnecessary, simplifying fashion, stripping away the excess. Simplicity is the keynote of all true elegance. But simplicity isn't easy to achieve. It's like sculpting, no? You must remove what doesn't serve the form. You must be bold enough to erase what others say is beautiful until you find what truly is.

"When I started designing, I was fed up with the day's fashion. Corsets, feathers, frills... women looked like they were carrying a garden on their heads. I thought, 'Why must we suffer to be considered beautiful?' I wanted freedom - for myself, for women. That is how I found my way."

And have you succeeded in your mission to free women through fashion?

"That's for others to say. But I believe that I succeeded because women understood what I was doing. The world was changing. After the war, women needed freedom. They worked, they smoked, and they drove cars. They weren't fragile dolls anymore. I just gave them what they needed.

When I introduced the little black dress in 1926, they called it 'Chanel's Ford.' Like a car, they said - a uniform for women. I didn't mind. I was making something that every woman could wear. Fashion should be accessible and should fit the life you live. Today, fashion is moving too fast. Trends come and go like the wind. But true style? It remains."

You also invented Chanel No. 5, the perfume that revolutionised fragrance. What inspired you to do that?

"No. 5. is a woman's perfume with a woman's scent, not the smell of flowers or a powder puff. It was 1921, and I wanted something revolutionary. I worked with Ernest Beaux, a brilliant perfumer. I told him: 'I want an aroma like a dress that evokes a woman, not a rose.' And then he gave me samples. I knew immediately that the fifth sample was the one. So, I called it No. 5 and five is a lucky number. I launched it on the fifth day of the fifth month of May. Everything aligned."

Even today, Coco, your Chanel No. 5, remains one of the best-selling perfumes in the world.

I almost miss a glint of pride in her eyes. "I created something eternal that women didn't know they wanted yet. That is the secret to all my success - I listen not to what they ask for, but what they need."

Although I know you don't like to dwell on your childhood, would you be willing to talk about it briefly?

"If we must. I was born Gabrielle Bonheur Chanel in 1883, and my early life was marked by hardship - my mother's death, my father's abandonment, and years in an orphanage run by nuns.

How do you think these events influenced your outlook?

"No one escapes such experiences unscathed. As you rightly say, I don't discuss my childhood much, but it gave me everything. My mother's death taught me the fragility of life. And the nuns taught me discipline. I learned how to sew from them. I learned to appreciate restraint. Discipline is freedom, you know. Once you control yourself, you can control the world. I became who I was because I refused to be a victim of my circumstances. You must fight for what you want. I refused to be poor. I refused to be ordinary."

This leads me to ask you about your love life. Although your many relationships are famous, you remain single. Did love play any role in your success?

She laughs softly, a sound both bitter and wistful. "Love? God knows I wanted love. But the moment I had to choose between the man I loved and my dresses, I chose the dresses. Work has always been a drug for me, even if I sometimes wonder what Chanel would have been without the men in my life.

Love played a role, yes. But not the way you think. 'Boy' Capel - he was my great love. We were made for each other. All that mattered was that he was there and loved me. And he knew that I loved him. Once, I said I was not pretty like his other women, and he said, "No, you're not, but I know no one more beautiful than you." He believed in me, but he didn't save me. No one saved me but myself." She pauses, flicking her cigarette.

And the Duke of Westminster?

"My relationship with the Duke was a significant part of my life in the 1920s. He was rich and helped shape my personal and professional life. He was charming, but I never wanted to be someone's wife. I don't belong to anyone. Not to a man, not to society. I belong to myself. A woman who marries her fortune marries her end."

In 1939, you made a difficult decision. You chose to close the House of Chanel.

"The world was at war, and fashion seemed irrelevant. France was torn apart, and I couldn't continue as if nothing had changed. So, I closed my doors. I thought my time was over and I'd done all I could. But fashion never dies, and neither do women's needs."

Yes, you stunned everyone with your comeback in 1954. After such a long absence, let's discuss what brought about Chanel's remarkable renaissance.

Her eyes light up at the memory: "I'll give you two reasons, both of which are true. Marlene Dietrich launched a second career in Las Vegas with her lovely throaty songs and wearing a slinky, near-transparent silk dress. After a fitting, Marlene asked me, "Why did you start up again?" I said, "Because I was bored to death." "You too?" said Marlene.

And what's the second reason that brought you back from having

retired so spectacularly at the start of World War Two?

"I couldn't stand by and watch women once again be imprisoned by fashion. Dior's 'New Look' - those corsets, those exaggerated skirts - were everything I had fought against. I returned because women needed me and because the world had forgotten how to dress with freedom. At the time, they called me old and outdated. But I knew they were wrong. Women wanted to feel free again, and I gave them what they needed."

What was the reaction to your comeback?

"Well, as I said, the critics were initially harsh. They claimed I'd lost touch and was disconnected from the current generation. Some even suggested I was irrelevant in a world I had once dominated. But I was confident fashion would find its way back to me. Deep down, I never believed those critics. I knew fashion would return to me, and it did. I trusted that true style is timeless. And trends, they come and go, eventually returning to their roots.

After the war, the world had changed so much. There was a sense of freedom and confusion. Women were starting to shed the ultra-feminine, restrictive styles of the 1950s, and they were hungry for something different. They needed clothes that allowed them to move, breathe, and feel empowered - not just in their homes but the world."

In other words, you resumed offering simplicity?

"Exactly. That's precisely what I gave them. The classic Chanel suit - a structured jacket, a skirt that allowed a woman to walk, to live. These were designs that defied the excess and impracticality of the times. Once again, I didn't give them what was expected. I gave them what they needed.

Of course, it wasn't easy. When I reopened my house in 1954, I entered a very different fashion world than the one I had left behind.

Christian Dior's 'New Look,' with nipped-in waists and full skirts, was beautiful yet nostalgic. It clung to a vision of womanhood that I felt was out of sync with the modern world. My designs were for the future. They were for the women who wanted more than just to be looked at and admired. They hungered to move, to act, to live."

Your comeback then wasn't just about fashion?

"No, it was about understanding women's lives and giving them a way to express their independence, strength, and sophistication. The Paris press was particularly unforgiving. They called me a relic of the past. But then something extraordinary happened. It wasn't the critics who validated me. It was the women themselves. They embraced my designs because they understood what I was doing. I wasn't just designing clothes. I was offering them a new way of being. I had always said that luxury must be comfortable; otherwise, it is not luxury. And finally, they were ready for that. They were tired of the constraints — both physical and societal. And so, they came back to me."

A flicker of nostalgia in her gaze: The truth is, I had been here before. When I started, everyone told me I was wrong, that women wanted to stay in their corsets and lace. But I knew better. I knew that women craved freedom. My designs have always been about liberation, from when I cut off the corset and gave women jersey dresses that moved with their bodies, not against them. This second time was no different.

My life has been about knowing who I am and what I stand for. Fashion, like life, is cyclical. I've always stayed true to my beliefs, and the world has eventually caught up. They say a woman who changes her principles depending on the time isn't a woman of principle. I never changed. And in the end, I didn't need to. Fashion came back to me because I never left it."

Thank you, Coco, for spending some time with me.

As I head for the door, Coco hands me a tiny bottle with clear liquid inside. "It's been a pleasure. I'd like you to have this small memento of our meeting. It's only a trial version, but I thought I'd have a go at creating an aroma just for men. Use it sparingly as you probably won't see it sold for quite a while."

NOTE: The Chanel company eventually launched several fragrances specifically aimed at men. One of the most iconic is Chanel No. 19, released in 1970 with both masculine and feminine elements. As I leave 31 Rue Cambon, I reflect on how Chanel's resilience outlasted many competitors. Her comeback wasn't just a return to fashion but a culmination of her life's work — rooted in her belief that style was not dictated by trends but by the spirit of the women who wore her clothes.

So much information is available on Coco Chanel that one is spoilt for choice. One of the best biographies and a great read, even if a bit dated, is Coco Chanel, by Alex Madsen, Bloomsbury 1990.

MARY PICKFORD

1892–1979

Mary Pickford, a Canadian-American film actress and producer, was one of early Hollywood's most famous and influential women. She was a founding member of United Artists and the Academy of Motion Picture Arts and Science.

"If you have made mistakes, even serious mistakes, there is always another chance for you."

MARY PICKFORD

Arriving in a studio car, I am about to embark on the exclusive experience of a conversation with the Queen of Hollywood, Mary Pickford. I am at the gates of the renowned mansion, Pickfair, which she shared with her equally illustrious husband, the actor Douglas Fairbanks.

Two stone pillars, with small gesturing statues on top, support elaborate wrought-iron gates. The design includes a large letter P for Pickfair. This place embodies Hollywood's golden age. It's a living monument to the era when Pickford and Fairbanks reigned supreme.

My heart quickens as the majestic gates swing slowly open, revealing the sprawling mansion whose scale and grandeur speak volumes of the era of Hollywood magnificence.

A butler greets me at the front door and guides me through several rooms, each seeming more lavish than the last. Finally, I arrive at the Grand Salon with its high, beamed ceilings and large French doors. These open onto a terrace on which I spot the silhouette of Mary Pickford. Beyond her lie superb views of the surrounding hills. She turns to greet me.

"Welcome to Pickfair. I'm so glad you could join me today."

Mary Pickford, it's an honour to speak with you.

She laughs softly, "Please, for heaven's sake, just call me Mary."

Thank you, Mary. Your contributions to the film industry are legendary, and I've come to hear your life story directly from your unique perspective.

"I'll do my best. Sharing my journey will be a pleasure." Then, waving to the surroundings: "You know I wasn't born to all this. Once, in the 1890s, I was just plain Gladys Louise Smith, living in Toronto, Canada, with my parents. My father passed away when I was very young. And my poor mother, Charlotte, struggled to support us. She took in boarders and did whatever she could to make ends meet. That early experience of hardship instilled in me a deep drive to succeed."

Can you describe the essentials? How did you get started in acting?

"It was pure luck! In 1899, my mother saw a notice seeking child actors and convinced me to audition despite my initial reluctance. Imagine! I was just five years old when I got my first role.

And what was that role, Mary?

It was in a short film called "The Violin Maker of Cremona." Naturally, it was silent, and I played only a minor part. We moved to New York City, where opportunities were more abundant. I began working on the stage, and by 1909, I had joined the Biograph Company, where I met D.W. Griffith."

That man - so controversial! Even so, he was a pivotal figure in early cinema. Tell me, Mary, what was it like working with him?

"Demanding. He was a real slave driver but a visionary who profoundly understood film as an art form. Under his ruthless direction, I learned so much about acting for the camera. He encouraged me to be natural and subtle. This style was quite different from the exaggerated gesturing typical of stage acting at that time. This experience was invaluable and set the foundations for my film career."

And you have become one of the first true movie stars. Can you talk about being in the spotlight during that silent era?

"It was exhilarating and challenging. In those days, we worked incredibly hard. I acted in multiple films simultaneously, sometimes working from dawn until dusk. But the recognition was gratifying. Fans would send letters by the thousands, and I felt a deep connection to my audience."

Yes, you'll forever be known as America's Sweetheart.

"That's been both a privilege and a responsibility. I have always taken my role as a public figure very seriously."

But your career hasn't been without its struggles. Can you tell me about some of the significant trials you faced?

"One of the hardest was breaking away from the studio system's control. Early on, actors had little say in their careers and were usually treated as mere commodities. This unfairness drove me to take control of my destiny. In 1919, along with Charlie Chaplin, D.W. Griffith, and Douglas Fairbanks, we co-founded United Artists, or UA as we came to call it. UA gave artists more control over their work, defying the tyrannical studio system.

That was groundbreaking. Your determination played a pivotal role in making it happen. How did it change the industry at that time?

"UA was a game-changer, allowing actual filmmakers to be their own bosses. It meant being free to produce the films of our choice and to retain creative control."

Can you explain the ramifications a bit more?

"Being able to select our projects, directors, and co-stars, we, the artists, could ensure the quality of our movies. This independence was crucial for artistic expression and set a precedent for future generations in Hollywood. It was one of my proudest achievements, though it only lasted a relatively short time."

What fascinates me about you, Mary, is that you became an accomplished businesswoman while still excelling in acting. How did you manage this transformation?

"With some difficulty! Apart from founding United Artists with shared creative control and profit participation, I also needed excellent negotiating skills, commercial awareness and…"

Hang on, Mary! Please tell me more about those widely admired negotiating skills!

"OK, I understand. Let's stick with the 1919 contract with Famous Players-Lasky, later Paramount Pictures. It involved a bruising form of bargaining with no holds barred on either side. But eventually, I got what I wanted, a salary of $10,000 a week, plus half of the film's profits."

My research found that this deal made you the highest-paid actress in Hollywood, setting a new standard for actor contracts. It must have felt exhilarating."

"We certainly celebrated Hollywood style, I can tell you."

You've also been highly active in what's now called branding and public relations.

"I suppose so. In those early days, I did a lot to hone my 'America's Sweetheart' image, which helped build a loyal fan base. And, of course, I used that popularity to gain better contracts and more significant roles."

Another aspect of your business approach is your keen eye for selecting scripts and projects. Can you talk briefly about that?

"I ensure that I'm always deeply involved in the production process. That way, the films I star in meet my high standards. This involvement means not only quality but long-term consistency in production."

Later, the rapid switch from silent to sound films was a huge mountain to climb. You emerged from it as one of the few great survivors.

"Nice of you to say that. You see, early on, I realised the importance of adapting to new technologies. While many of my silent film star colleagues struggled to cope with talkies, I embraced the switch, which seemed perfectly sensible. As a result, I began producing sound films, many of which proved successful."

It's easy to admire your business acumen, but you also actively give back to the community.

"Yes, I suppose so. I'm involved in various charitable activities and am one of the founders of the Motion Picture Relief Fund. The fund plays a vital role in supporting industry workers in need. "

Your initiative has undoubtedly helped others and enhanced your reputation as a compassionate leader.

"Guilty as charged!"

In addition to all that, Mary, you've also worked with almost everyone famous and notorious in Hollywood. Can you share some of your more memorable incidents or interactions?

"There are so many! One that stands out is my friendship with Charlie Chaplin. We had a deep mutual respect and a playful rivalry. I remember a time during the making of The Poor Little Rich Girl when he visited the set. Charlie couldn't resist giving me irrelevant tips on slapstick comedy when my role was more dramatic. Yet his presence always brought a spark of creativity and joy.

Another memorable time was working with Douglas Fairbanks, whom I later married. Our collaboration on "The Thief of Bagdad" in 1924 showcased Fairbanks's extraordinary athleticism and charisma and highlighted his innovative approach to filmmaking. I admired his innate ability to merge spectacle with narrative, a characteristic that set new standards in the industry."

Also, of course, you held lavish parties together here at Pickfair.

They weren't just social occasions. They were also a way to share artistic ideas and where ideas flowed freely among the brightest and best of the film industry. Fairbanks's charisma and charm had an almost magical ability to create an atmosphere that encouraged creativity and camaraderie.

Your romantic and legendary union captivated the public's imagination and symbolised the glamour and charisma of the silent film era.

"Yes, I agree. My husband Douglas was born in 1883, and when our paths crossed, he was already a charismatic and athletic actor known for his swashbuckling roles in silent films like The Mark of Zorro and The Thief of Bagdad, which I've already mentioned.

His dynamic screen presence and daring stunts earned him the nickname King of Hollywood. Poor Douglas lost a legal battle over some of his excellent early films. The judge said he was just an employee with no rights in these productions. That awful situation stimulated me to purchase fifty of my original films with the Biograph company to prevent the same thing from happening to me. Chaplin, of course, did much the same, retaining tight control over almost everything he did.

So, when did your much-publicised romance with Douglas begin?

"It started in the early 1910s when we were drawn to each other as kindred spirits and equals in an industry where such partnerships were rare. Douglas proposed to me uniquely and humorously. I was on a tennis court when he arranged for a plane to fly overhead with a banner that read, "Mary, will you marry me?"

That must have been quite a shock.

"Do you know, I didn't even notice the banner at first as I was so focused on the game? When I finally did, I was overwhelmed with joy and immediately said yes. We began several collaborative projects, including, of course, founding United Artists."

Mary, you and your husband became known as Hollywood's first so-called power couple, and Pickfair became a social hub for the industry.

"It's been marvellous hosting legends like Rudolph Valentino, Lillian Gish, and Albert Einstein. Our gatherings were always filled with lively discussions about art, science, and the future of cinema."

The story of your life always sounds straight from a Hollywood script. What lessons have you gained from that script that you could share with others aspiring to succeed?

As if mentally consulting a secret manual, Mary nods: "I've learned several important lessons. First, resilience is crucial. Life will always throw obstacles your way, and how you respond to them matters and defines your success. Never give up, no matter how tough things get.

Second, don't wait for opportunities to come to you; create them. Be proactive in your career, and never be afraid to stand up for what you believe in. Third, trust your instincts and be sure to remain authentic. People quickly detect when you're not being genuine. Even when it's hard, stay true to yourself and your values. Lastly, never stop learning. The world is constantly changing, so it's vital to remain curious and adaptable.

Those are powerful lessons, Mary. Thank you. Since you starred in approximately 52 feature films and all those short ones from the silent era, the total must be well over 200. Is there one film that is very special to you? One that you're most proud of?

"I am so pleased you asked me that question. I have a small surprise for you. Please come with me."

To my total delight, this remarkable woman takes hold of my hand and gently leads me to the nearby entrance of her private cinema. The double doors reveal a comfy yet opulent room with plush red velvet seats. An ornate ceiling and a state-of-the-art projector set the stage for an unforgettable experience. We sit in the front row, and the lights dim. The projector whirs into life, casting a golden beam across the room.

Instantly, I am transported back to the silent film era when Mary Pickford reigned supreme. The screen flickers with scenes from Sparrows, a hauntingly beautiful 1926 film. Transfixed, I watch as Mary's film character, a brave and resourceful girl called Molly, leads a group of orphans through harrowing trials on a lonely farm. Her captivating performance confirms her immense talent and dedication.

As the final credits roll on this silent masterpiece, and the lights brighten, a more profound silence descends. In the dim light, I glimpse Mary with an intense expression. "Sparrows was a labour of love. It wasn't just about entertaining people. It showed the strength and resilience of the human spirit, especially in the face of adversity. Sparrows is far more than a film to me. It's a piece of my soul."

You've granted me an experience I'll never forget, Mary; thank you so much for sharing it with me.

She gently presses my hand: "And thank you for reminding me that my work still touches people's hearts."

NOTE: Despite the eventual dissolution of their marriage, Mary Pickford and Douglas Fairbanks' legacy endures. They are remembered for their remarkable contributions to cinema and influence on Hollywood's social and cultural landscape. Their romance remains emblematic of the golden age of Hollywood when the stars shone brightly, and the allure of their lives captivated the world.

An excellent biography is Mary Pickford by Scott Eyman, Robson Books, 1992.

BARBARA HEPWORTH

1903–1975

A renowned British sculptor, her modernist works in stone, wood, and bronze are celebrated for their organic forms and harmonious design. As a leading figure in 20th-century art, she helped redefine sculpture, and her approach and values remain influential in shaping abstract art worldwide.

"I am always striving for the simplicity of form. so that it can express both the inner and outer life."

Interview with British art critic and historian Anthony Caro, 1960.

BARBARA HEPWORTH

We meet by appointment in St Ives, Cornwall, in late 1965. This acclaimed sculptress has lived happily here in the Trewyn Studio and Garden for over a decade. The Cornish coastal air and rugged landscape provide a perfect backdrop for her art.

She arrives wearing her characteristic informal, zipped working jacket for our conversation. She greets me with a particularly strong handshake and a friendly smile, and we walk into her studio, where we settle down to talk.

First, thank you, Ms Hepworth, for sparing time from your current project, which I can see from here is awaiting your attention.

"Glad we can meet today. How can I help you?"

Your art stands on its own and needs no patronising approval by the rest of the world. Yet, your well-deserved recent Order of the British Empire once more confirms your influence and broader recognition.

"That's most kind of you to say so. Please call me Barbara. The real reward is not the medal. It's the creation of the art itself. My main concern is always achieving impact with my work rather than gaining accolades or, as you say, winning further external recognition."

Let's then start at the beginning. I know you were born in 1903 in Wakefield, Yorkshire. What was it like growing up there, and how did that place shape your artistic journey?

"Yes, I come from Yorkshire, and its landscape has never entirely left me. Growing up surrounded by hills, nature's shapes and curves had a decisive long-term influence."

Your parents?

"My father was an engineer, which also influenced me. I loved watching how things were constructed , and the various material shapes came together. The land and the engineering, the organic and the mechanical, inspire how I view form."

From what you've just said and written elsewhere, it seems that by the time you reached your teenage years, you had already decided to become a sculptor. Is that right?

"True. I won a scholarship to attend Leeds School of Art, where I met Henry Moore. We were later grouped as part of the modernist movement. But though we had similar interests, my artistic vision differed from his."

What did you think of sculpture as an art form in those early days?

"I saw sculpture, and still do, as a way to communicate deep emotional responses. It channels primal human instincts into physical form."

Was this in tune with Moore, with whom you were studying?

"Absolutely. Henry and I had a strong connection from the start. But we were always highly independent in our thinking. The popular press tended to link us with one another, which was wrong since sculpture is very personal. For me, it's always about communicating my sense of the world. Early on, I began exploring stone carving, which became a critical part of my practice."

Why stone? What drew you to this most demanding medium?

"Stone is honest with a life of its own. Carving the material is a way of working with that life rather than imposing something on it. When you carve, you reveal what's inside. You don't create something entirely new, and I love that it's a dialogue between the material and the artist."

Wasn't that how Michelangelo regarded it, too? He was famous for saying, "I saw the angel in the marble and carved until I set him free."

"Exactly, the role of a sculptor is merely to liberate the forms trapped inside the marble, not as someone imposing a shape on an otherwise unformed block."

As I understand it, Barbara, this dialogue between you and the stone led you to become committed to "direct carving," working with the material immediately rather than first creating preparatory models.

"Correct. During the late 1920s, while travelling through Italy on a scholarship, I became fully immersed in direct carving techniques. My passion for this way of working was not merely a technical decision."

What do you mean: it was not merely a technical decision? Can you elaborate on that, please?

"It was ideological. Sculpture, like life, should evolve organically, not be dictated by preconceived plans."

You once said: "There's something pure about working directly with the material."

"Yes, rather than forcing an idea onto it, let the material guide you, shape your vision. For example, I rarely draw what I see. I draw what I feel in my body."

Please tell me more about that trip to Italy. That must have been most stimulating for a young artist.

Her eyes light up at the memory, and her speech almost imperceptibly reverts to her Yorkshire origins. "Oh, Italy was especially transformative. The Renaissance artists, their understanding of form, space, and the landscape and the light! It's so very different from Yorkshire, but it similarly touched me. There's something ancient about both places, a connection to the earth."

What else does Italy mean to you?

"I married my first husband there, my fellow artist John Skeaping. When we returned to England in 1929, I had my first child, Paul.

Unfortunately, things didn't work out between John and me. Later, I met the painter Ben Nicholson, who became my second husband and a creative collaborator."

Can you discuss your working relationship with Nicholson?

"Ben and I had a most stimulating partnership. He was deeply involved in developing abstract art in Britain, and his way of seeing the world resonated with me. We worked in parallel, though I wouldn't say we directly influenced each other. It was more that we were both moving in the same direction, exploring abstraction and form in our own ways.

Nicholson introduced me to a world of sharp lines and geometric purity. However, I wanted my forms to retain a softness and sensuality. I've always been more interested in curves, the tension between soft and hard, balance and imbalance."

Reconciling those opposing forces makes so many of your sculptures memorable. Since we're talking about Nicholson, you continued collaborating with him during the 1930s. With war on the horizon, how did these two factors impact your work at the time?

"Inevitably, personal and global factors impacted my work, which consequently acquired a new emotional depth and reflected those tensions. As a family, we moved to Cornwall trying to shelter from the chaos of war in the peace and isolation of St Ives."

Surrounded here by the sea and the wild landscape, you've created some of your most celebrated work. Specifically, how do you think the environment here influences your sculpture? It's such a dramatic place.

"I don't think I could have produced the same work elsewhere. Cornwall has a rawness and purity. The sea, the rocks, the wind... you feel connected to something larger than yourself. That connection is what I try to bring into my sculptures. That is, something elemental, a universal form."

Again, can you elaborate on this Barbara?

"Well, many of my sculptures echo the contours of the Cornish landscape. It makes them more organic with rounded forms. Pierced holes became a new important element. These openings allow light and air to flow through the sculptures. They create a new dynamic interaction between the piece, the environment, and the viewer."

You have been pretty isolated here in Cornwall, especially in the early days. I realise that was partly deliberate, but how does self-imposed isolation help your work?

"It's not just an aesthetic experience, this isolation. Through the experience, I began to see my sculptures as not merely objects of beauty but as entities in themselves."

What does that mean, Barbara?

"My work naturally interacts with the world surrounding them, like how Cornwall's landscapes interact with the elements."

Pierced holes are an essential element of your art. For many who admire your work, they have a fascination all of their own. What do they represent for you?

"It's a good question. I think of the holes as portals. They're a way of opening space and creating a sense of infinity within a solid form. We touched on this issue earlier. It's about balancing mass and void, between the tangible and the intangible."

Can we now explore what it means to be a sculptor? For many non-sculptors, such as myself, sculpting is one of the most physically and mentally demanding activities one can do for a living.

"That's true; It's no easy route to travel! But for the artist, there first must be an innate compulsion, something unavoidable rather than a choice. In essence, the material itself guides the sculpting practice. As the recipient of that compulsion and responding to the needs of the material, I experience intense pleasure in creating a new form that conveys my feelings.

Let me put it this way: I see sculpture as channelling primal human instincts into human form. You must do some sculpture to know its spirit. Sculptural understanding can't be theoretical or learned from books."

We've already touched on the artistic challenges of balancing different forces in your work. However, the sheer practicalities of having a young son and then giving birth to triplets in the early 1930s must have been highly demanding for you and your husband.

"Having children is an incredible privilege. There's nothing like sculpting with a child sitting on your knee or working through the night when they're asleep. Do you know I carved some of my best work when the triplets were tiny?"

Given the limited support systems for working mothers, balancing your family life with your work must have been incredibly challenging. How did you and your husband cope?

"Ben was deeply engaged in his artistic career. He didn't provide much practical support in parenting. His focus remained largely on his own work."

Typical! Then and now, many women face the challenge of maintaining their careers while taking on a disproportionate share of childcare. From what you say, Ben's primary focus on his work left you with much parental responsibility. How did this impact your creative process?

"Surprisingly, as I said, I did some of my best work then. For example, the Oval Form series and Pelagos."

Yes, these have become celebrated for their lyrical abstraction.

"Yes, they meant a lot to me, even though it took many long nights to complete them while doing childcare."

In 1950, you represented Britain at the Venice Biennale. For any artist, that was a significant achievement. What was it like for you?

"It was a pivotal moment. Honestly, though, I've never thought of my work in terms of national pride. For me, sculpture is universal. It speaks to all people, regardless of nationality. Still, it was wonderful to be part of that conversation on an international stage."

So, in what way did the Biennale experience affect your later work?

"Well, to my delight, there was a definite increase in work requested for larger public commissions. One of my most significant pieces from that time was Contrapuntal Forms. Working large is always challenging, but I love its freedom. It helps me to think about the work and its surroundings. That is, how people will move around it and how it interacts with light and weather. It's like creating a living entity. With Contrapuntal Forms, I wanted to express a sense of harmony between the two elements moving in concert."

Another of your most famous works is the 21-foot-tall Single Form commission, outside the United Nations headquarters in New York in 1964. How did this come about, and what does that piece represent to you?

"That sculpture was in praise of Dag Hammarskjöld, the second Secretary-General of the United Nations. He tragically died in a plane crash in 1961 while on a peacekeeping mission in Africa. Dag was a dear friend, and his death affected me deeply.

I wanted to create something that embodied the ideals for which he stood: peace, unity, and strength. Single Form is, therefore, a tribute to him. But it's also a statement about the power of sculpture to communicate on a global scale."

The work undoubtedly confirmed your reputation as a sculptor of international stature. Its sheer scale, combined with its symbolic resonance, marked your entry into monumental art.

"I agree. It's one thing to create for galleries or small outdoor spaces. Creating something that speaks on such a large, public stage is quite another. You have to think about the audience differently. How will the work be perceived by people who pass it every day? How can it maintain its relevance over time?"

You've lived through so much. Two world wars, the rise of modernism and, of course, the women's movement. How do you see your place in all of them?

Hepworth pauses to consider her response. "I've never thought of myself as part of any particular movement. I've always been guided by a desire to understand the world through form. I don't think about whether I'm a woman or a British sculptor. I think about what it means to be human, to experience life, and how I can translate that into my work."

Still, you've navigated a field historically dominated by men, breaking through many barriers to establish yourself as a leading figure in modern sculpture.

"It was difficult at times. Only some people took women sculptors seriously, especially in the early days. But I never let that distract me from my work. I always believed that the art would speak for itself, which it has done."

Yes, that's true, Barbara. And we can't end our conversation without discussing your studio garden here and how it's evolved into a living extension of your creativity. How do you see this space continuing to influence your future work?

"Well, yes, I constantly think about its development and how it opens up new artistic possibilities. My friend Priaulx Rainier helped me transform the garden, using her knowledge of plants from her native South Africa. It feels as if I've been laying my roots here along with the roots of the trees. One day, perhaps this place can become a public space. Also, the plants here grow so prolifically I may have to give up sculpture to attend them!"

One last question. What advice would you give to aspiring artists today?

Hepworth takes a deep breath, leaning forward to answer with great intensity. "I would say—don't be afraid to follow your instincts. There's so much pressure to conform, especially when starting. But if you can remain true to your vision and world experience, that's where the real art comes from. Like any art, sculpture is about discovering and pushing boundaries, both of the material and yourself."

Her eyes drift to the nearby half-finished piece from which I have enticed her to have this meeting. "And don't be afraid to fail. Some of my best work came after periods of struggle or doubt. You must learn to trust the process, even when it is difficult. Be willing to fully immerse yourself in the work, live and breathe it. That's where the absolute joy comes from. The work is not separate from life; it's an extension."

You've been so generous with your time today, Barbara; I'll finally let you get back to the work calling for you. Thank you so much.

NOTE: Her influence goes beyond her creations. The Hepworth legacy can be seen in countless contemporary artists who draw on her ideas of space, form, and materiality. Her work continues to inspire sculptors, architects, landscape designers, and even philosophers who find a profound meditation on existence in her art.

In one sense, Hepworth's sculptures are immortal. They speak to the fundamental human experience and will continue to resonate as long as people yearn for connection, balance, and meaning.

After she died in 1975, her family, following her wishes, gifted her home and studio in St Ives, Cornwall, along with the garden, to the nation. This happened in 1976, a year after her passing. Today, the Tate Gallery manages its care and preservation. It remains a delightful place to visit and showcase her sculptures in their natural setting. The museum and garden are vital to Hepworth's legacy and open to the public.

For more about this remarkable woman, check out Barbara Hepworth, The Sculptor in the Studio by Sophie Bowness, Tate Publishing

GRACE HOPPER

1906–1992

An American computer scientist, mathematician, and US Navy Rear Admiral, Grace Hopper pioneered computer programming. She was the first to devise the theory of machine-independent programming languages. Using it, she developed COBOL in the late 1950s, a language that remains used today. Grace also wrote the first computer manual, a significant contribution that laid the foundation for modern computing.

"The most dangerous phrase in the language is, 'We've always done it this way."

Grace Hopper and the Invention of the Information Age by Kurt Beyer, 2009

GRACE HOPPER

It's early October 1985, in the heart of Washington, D.C., and the tech world is starting to bubble with innovation. I have come to these grand yet pleasant Naval Data Automation Command offices to meet Rear Admiral Grace Hopper, sometimes known as "Amazing Grace." She's as busy as ever, working where technology and the military intersect at the dawn of the digital age.

After passing through security, I am taken to a stark, somewhat soulless meeting room where Grace awaits. She's wearing her signature Navy uniform, complete with the insignia of her rank and a cluster of ribbon bars, the colourful representations of the prestigious medals and honours she has earned. The most recent addition is the National Medal of Technology, awarded for her pioneering work in computer science.

From an adjacent room, there's a persistent hum of computer terminals. They are an appropriate backdrop for meeting this remarkable person. Staring hard at me, this formidable expert drums her fingers on the table, suggesting she's impatient to begin our conversation.

Admiral Hopper, thank you for speaking with me today; I'm most honoured.

"Happy to help. What exactly would you like to talk about?"

Many people know about your computer science work, yet few understand how it began. What first sparked your interest in mathematics and computing?

"It all started as a small girl with my insatiable curiosity. When I was seven, I took one of our alarm clocks to pieces before my mother realised what I was doing. When I tried putting it back together again, nothing worked. So, I found seven more of our clocks and dismantled them too. When I deconstructed the final one, I finally understood how they worked. After that, my mother limited me to one clock.

My mother also had a deep love for math and science. For her generation, though, opportunities for women in those fields were almost non-existent. Yet, she was a constant source of encouragement. I found her determination to overcome gender barriers inspiring.

Another strong influence was my father. He was a civil engineer and a lifelong learner who believed in pushing boundaries. He felt there was no limit to what his daughter could achieve, which was progressive thinking for his time. He and my mother made sure that I developed a strong sense of independence and determination. Their support gave me the courage to pursue a path uncommon for women back then."

Does family life appeal to you, or do computers rule your existence?

"My family life has been unconventional. In the 1930s, I married a professor, but it didn't work out, and we divorced in 1945. We had no children, so I poured myself into my work. The people I work with have become my family. The Navy is my extended family, and I have never remarried.

Mathematics gave me a sense of control over complex systems. There's a beauty to numbers and the logic behind them. Mathematics has always felt like a language that could explain the world to me."

What drew you to computers that were then so little understood?

"It started when I was a professor of mathematics at Vassar, the Vassar College in Poughkeepsie, New York. When World War II started, I was asked to work on a huge new computer at Harvard. I had no idea how much that decision would change my life. Computers then were far from what we have today, yet from the moment our paths crossed, I knew it was the future."

What was it like working on that giant machine?

"Stunning. This monster was fifty feet long, eight feet tall, and packed with clanking switches, relays, and countless moving parts. It was like a massive, mechanical brain, and I was in awe. It was the most complex, unique computing machine ever created. Nor did I know how you talked to it since the thing didn't understand English. There were no instructions or guidebooks.

Can you explain what this giant machine was actually for?

"Yes, of course. Our giant toy was a new type of secret weapon and one that could change the war's outcome. We used it to calculate solutions for rocket trajectories, proximity fuses and mines. We also generated tables of mathematical functions that could be used to solve general engineering problems."

There's a legend that when that early giant machine crashed, you evolved a word to describe what happened, and it's still used today.

"It's no legend. But let me give you a bit of background on that well-worn tale. I was a little bewildered and thoroughly scared when I arrived to work on this device. IBM, the makers hadn't got around to installing smooth steel casing. Instead, all the 750,000 parts were fully exposed to view.

Meanwhile, I'd been given a simple math problem and needed the machine to help solve it quickly. So, you can imagine the impact when, one day, without warning, that monster stopped. The device quite simply ground to a halt. We were desperate to discover what had gone wrong, but no one could find why. We almost took the thing apart, searching for the cause.

Then, someone spotted a moth stuck in one of those essential relays among the 3,500 electromechanical relays, 2,300 storage counters, and thousands of back-wired relay terminals, all controlled by a unique three-inch wide punch tape. The now dead insect had caused the failure. We extracted it and stuck the insect into the logbook with a note saying we had 'debugged' the machine. That's how the term came into use, and ever since, we've always been fixing glitches or bugs."

A great story, Admiral. Speaking of legends, how did you go on to create one of the most powerful programming languages?

"Mmm, that's a good question. How can I put it? In the earliest days, we communicated with a computer using special codes. If you wanted to work with a new machine, guess what? The previous instructions were useless, and you had to rewrite everything from scratch. It was most inefficient.

I had this wild idea that we could create a new form of instruction close to standard English. That way, non-mathematicians could use the latest code too. At first, people said I was out of my mind. They said, 'Computers can't understand English!' But I didn't see why not."

And what did this mean in practical terms?

Grace smiles at the thought: "This new language could run on any suitable machine and was easy to understand. And, well, the rest is history!"

Do you mean because it ended up being a sort of universal language?

"Exactly. Even now, millions of lines of that code are still running worldwide. It's incredible that what we built back then has stood the test of time. Of course, it's evolved, but the principles remain the same."

Excellent. Pushing through the initial resistance must have taken determination.

"Oh boy, there was plenty of resistance, let me tell you! But I learned early on that if you believe in something, you must fight for it. I've always lived by the motto, 'Do it first and apologise later!' I tended to ask for forgiveness rather than permission."

So, tell me about the resistance you encountered. Was it because people disliked change or because you were a woman?

"Another good question. Many people hated the idea of a woman leading such a revolutionary idea in a male-dominated field. But I wasn't going to let that stop me. One of the keys to my success was my sheer stubbornness. Whenever people put rocks in my path and told me 'no,' I worked even harder to prove them wrong. You have to have a thick skin in this line of work."

What other obstacles did you face as a woman working in the military and the tech world?

"There have been so many obstacles right from the start. Because of my age, they turned me down when I first tried to join the Navy in World War II. At 34, they said I was too old and skinny to enlist!"

How did you react to that prejudice?

"I didn't let that stop me. Instead, I joined the Naval Reserve with the Bureau of Ships, where I got my start on that first giant computer."

Still, being a woman in computing must have been an enormous challenge.

"It sure was. Few women were in high-ranking positions, especially in the Navy or corporate leadership. Sometimes, I was the only woman in the room. People underestimated me and assumed I was there to take notes or make coffee. But I always believed in myself and my ideas.

It's astonishing how far we've come. When I started, computers filled entire rooms and could only manage basic arithmetic. Now, we've ever smaller ones, which are many times more powerful. Back in the 1940s and 1950s, computers were mysterious, inaccessible machines. Today, anyone can learn to program, build software, or contribute to technological innovation.

The internet will transform many aspects of modern life. However, right now, it's still early. Another new idea is that machines can learn from data and make decisions. That's now the stuff of science fiction, but I guess it will happen. We must ensure that we use these technologies for the betterment of humanity."

Looking back on your spectacular career, things have not always gone smoothly. Have they? In 1949, for example, you found a new home working for a start-up computer company and threw your energies into helping it succeed.

"You've certainly done your homework! Yes, when things started to go wrong at the company, it caused me great distress. A previous alcohol addiction resurfaced. I'm not proud of what happened, but I was in a desperate physical and psychological state. I even suffered bouts of wanting to commit suicide. It nearly ended my career. But thankfully, sometimes, one's darkest moments in life become the catalyst for change, creating a foundation for future success.

The Remington Rand company took over the dying company. This was the start of one of my career's most productive and creative chapters. I became deeply involved with computer programming and devised innovative solutions."

You've always been forward-thinking. What is the most valuable lesson you draw for future generations from your career?

Hopper pauses to give the question her undivided attention: "It's to stay curious and keep learning. Technology keeps changing, which means being willing to do the same. There were no roadmaps when I started, and no one showed me the way forward. We had to figure it out as we went along, and that spirit of discovery drives innovation.

But more than that, I would say, don't be afraid to take risks. Don't fear challenging the status quo or trying something others say is impossible. The most significant innovations arise from pushing boundaries and breaking a few rules."

Now that you have done so much, Grace, what of your future?

The Admiral chuckles: "I've never been one for slowing down, as you might have guessed. Since retiring from the Navy, they keep calling me back, asking for my help."

You've said you don't believe in retirement, so how do you imagine you'll spend your time in the future?

"Oh, I don't imagine I'll ever stop since I want to spend more time mentoring and lecturing."

Your lectures and talks on computers are famous for being stimulating, what's the secret?

"I love communicating technological concepts in simple, engaging ways. For instance, I use a 30-centimeter wire to show how far an electrical signal travels in a nanosecond. It's tangible and helps people grasp what might otherwise seem abstract. I want to inspire that curiosity in others that has always driven me."

Finally, Admiral Hopper, is there one piece of advice that reflects the spirit of your life's work?

"Never stop asking questions. Don't be afraid to challenge what's in front of you. The world doesn't change by staying comfortable or sticking to what's easy. It changes when people step out of line and push boundaries. Don't let someone tell you something is impossible; go and do it. You might surprise yourself with what you're capable of."

Reaching into her handbag, the Admiral hands me a small object, explaining: "This little contraption is a backwards-running clock. It's a reminder of our time together and that time is not just linear. It's filled with opportunities to reflect and learn from our past. Looking at time this way, you're encouraged to think critically about your decisions and how they shape the future. It's a nudge to analyse mistakes, celebrate victories, and recognise patterns that can inform your path ahead."

I'm overwhelmed, Grace; this is an astonishing and thoughtful gift.

"It's a souvenir of our Conversation because I believe in the power of curiosity and learning. Like programming, life is about iteration - finding what works and what doesn't. I have used this little gadget sometimes as a tool for reflection. It can inspire you to look back, learn, and innovate. Remember, it's not just about where you're going, but also understanding where you've been."

Suddenly, the hum of the nearby machines stops. Grace is already on her feet: "I need to check out what's happening next door. Thanks for our conversation; I've enjoyed it. Goodbye."

As Grace exits, I recall she is no longer responsible for the nearby computer room; she's just intensely intrigued to learn more. Curiosity seems to sum up this remarkable woman.

NOTE: The U.S. Navy Arleigh Burke-class guided-missile destroyer USS Hopper and the Cray XE6 "Hopper" supercomputer were named after her. During her lifetime, she was awarded forty honorary degrees from universities worldwide, and a college at Yale University was renamed in her honour. In 1992, her passing marked the end of an era, but her legacy continues to influence and inspire.

For a full biography of Hopper, check out Grace Hopper and the Invention of the Information Age" by Kurt Beyer, MIT Press 2012.

RACHEL CARSON

1907–1964

Rachel Carson was an American marine biologist and conservationist. Her best-selling book Silent Spring almost single-handedly advanced the global environmental movement. Her work highlighted the dangers of pesticides, particularly DDT, leading to widespread ecological reforms.

"The more clearly we can focus our attention on the wonders and realities of the universe about us, the less taste we shall have for destruction."

Rachel Carson, Silent Spring, 1962

RACHEL CARSON

This is a quiet, unspoiled beach along the coast of Maine in 1962; Rachel Carson spends as much time here as she can. The sounds of the ocean, the scent of salt air, and the peaceful environment make this an ideal spot to discuss her observations of the natural world and its degradation. I will shortly have a conversation with one of the most influential figures in American and world ecological history.

Rachel sits beside me on this near-deserted beach. **Thank you for agreeing to meet me; I'm aware of your understandable resistance to being interviewed yet again. I know that you strongly reject playing the celebratory game, Rachel Carson.**

"Just 'Rachel', please. I'm happy to have an informal chat. At least there are no photographers with their flashing bulbs and instructions to look this way or that."

Yes, of course, Rachel. Can you tell me about your early years and how the natural world became so central to your life?

"Yes, I'm glad to talk about such a beautiful time of my life. I was lucky enough to enjoy a delightful childhood immersed in nature. I grew up in Springdale, a small Pennsylvania town where my mother encouraged a love for the outdoors. Living on a small farm, I spent countless hours exploring woods, fields, and streams. My mother's guidance about nature has coloured my whole life and given me a deep and abiding love for the natural world.

From a young age, I was hooked on telling stories alongside my love for nature. By the time I was ten, I'd already set my sights on becoming a writer. But, sadly, I found that I didn't have much imagination. Instead, biology has given me something to write about. As I matured, my fascination with nature and science took over. This led me to a degree in biology at Pennsylvania College for Women and later a master's degree in zoology from Johns Hopkins University."

What specifically inspired you to write about the sea?

"I had never even laid eyes on the sea in those early days. Then, after reading Alfred Lord Tennyson's poem Locksley Hall, I became convinced that the sea was my destiny. There was nothing rational about that revelation, and to this day, I can't fully explain how I knew where my newfound love of science would one day lead. I had yet to make the sea's acquaintance."

Tennyson's poem contains numerous unpleasant things. Despite these negatives, you chose to extract from it the importance of the sea.

"I did because that was where my entire focus was."

That intense focus has led you to become known as one of the most prominent female scientists. What challenges did you face as a woman pursuing a career in science?

"First, I should clarify that I have never worked as a scientist. In college, very few women were encouraged to pursue science work. Second, my family faced numerous financial difficulties. While studying, I had to take on any jobs, whatever I could get, making my academic journey more demanding. At Johns Hopkins, where I did my master's in zoology, I often felt oppressed by being one of the very few women in my field. But I kept going, and these obstacles only fuelled my determination. I hope my story can inspire others to overcome similar troubles."

Did you have any help tackling these problems?

"Luckily, mentors supported me and encouraged my scientific aspirations. After my father passed away in 1935, I became the primary breadwinner for my family. I put my doctoral studies on hold and got work with the U.S. Fish and Wildlife Service. While there, I wrote radio scripts for an educational series called Romance Under the Waves. That's when my writing and scientific careers began to merge."

That seems an understatement, Rachel! Didn't you actually go on to produce several bestsellers? Please tell me about these.

"My first book was Under the Sea-Wind in 1941, but no, it wasn't an immediate bestseller. It offered an unusual lyrical exploration of ocean life, blending science and poetic prose. I introduced readers to the intricacies of marine ecosystems and how delicately balanced they are. Then came The Sea Around Us in 1951, in which I took a complete look at oceanography and discussed the sea's physical and biological aspects."

Yes, I remember it showcased your genius for making science come so alive that your readers often didn't think of it as science.

"It's kind of you to say that. Achieving that involved searching the often dry and exceedingly technical papers of scientists for the kernels of facts to weave into my profile of the sea. My information came from more than a thousand sources, and scores of experts volunteered their thoughts and insights."

The Sea Around Us received praise for its engaging writing and scientific accuracy, sold two hundred thousand copies and won the National Book Award. You must have been thrilled.

"I was, and the reception encouraged me to make progress with the third in the series The Edge of the Sea, 1955. For that book, I examined the intertidal zone, focusing on the relationships between marine organisms and their environments. It also continued my approach of combining scientific research with accessible storytelling."

Writing something so substantial must have taken a long time, Rachel.

"It certainly did, but I was totally committed. I personally explored lots of places along the Atlantic seaboard. Everywhere I stopped, I recorded the look of the shore and the sea, how the wind felt, what the surf sounded like and how the sky and sand appeared. In my mind's eye, these coastal forms merge and blend in shifting, kaleidoscopic patterns without end. There is no ultimate and fixed reality; the earth can become as fluid as the sea itself."

This was your most personal presentation, drawing directly from your daily fieldwork. It felt like you were taking me by the hand as we explored the seashore together.

"I'm delighted that's your reaction, given how hard I had to work on this approach. The book's reception was really gratifying and made it all worthwhile."

I am not surprised! The New York Times critic declared: "Carson has done it again," and that your new book was "wise and wonderful." It joined the New York Times bestseller list like your previous one. Some journalists got so carried away with your lyrical writing that one even called you Washington's "newest glamour girl."

"Ghastly! These misguided enthusiasts took the book for granted and didn't realise it demanded countless hours and months to compose and needed endless revisions over and over and over. It was a labour of love, but the result was very hard won."

And there was much more to come. Can you explain what you did in your later campaigning and writing?

"First, let me tell you a story. While walking through quiet woodlands one day, I suddenly realised something was very wrong. I could hardly hear any birds. It was as if nature had gone silent. Then, in the late 1950s, I noticed alarming environmental patterns, particularly regarding the widespread use of pesticides like DDT. This realisation became the seed for my next book, Silent Spring, where I set out to challenge the status quo. I wanted to reveal the dark side of chemical use in agriculture."

Rachel, you did far more than produce a book with facts, statistics and science. It was unlike anything you'd previously written.

"Well, I knew I must captivate my readers with a compelling message based on meticulous research and lyrical prose. I set out to transform complex scientific information into powerful narratives. I painted vivid images of nature's interconnectedness. I urged people to consider the consequences of their actions on the environment."

Tracing even some of those connections must have taken a massive amount of research.

"Yes, I have always been concerned about being strictly accurate in my science writing. I gradually built a network of experts that I could consult. When one person agreed to help, I asked them to introduce me to one of their contacts and so on."

Your Silent Spring book took four arduous years to complete and had fifty-five pages of source citations and references. But when you finally released it in 1962, it won massive acclaim and produced a fierce backlash.

"As I expected. Yes, powerful chemical companies felt threatened by my findings. They launched a campaign to discredit me, labelling me an alarmist, a woman out of her depth."

But manifestly, you were not out of your depth.

"Well, I knew the truth of what I was writing. It wasn't just about me; it was about our planet and the future. To the fury of the chemical gang helping to destroy our planet, I keep speaking at conferences, engaging with scientists and policymakers, and continuing to write about my concerns."

This natural ability to connect with the public has been extraordinary. People generally reacted positively to your message, didn't they?

"Yes, they were hungry for information about the world around them. They wanted to be informed, and knowledge is a powerful catalyst for change. Finally, the government got in on the act and produced a detailed research report virtually vindicating my findings.

Silent Spring was reviewed everywhere. Over seventy newspapers ran editorials on it and chose to publish extracts. The book sold over five hundred thousand copies and started a "national quarrel."

"It's true. I felt by then that I had managed to draw attention to a serious flaw in how our society uses and abuses chemicals."

So, what do you see as your main message to the world?

"My message to the world is simple. We must reverse course or continue at our peril. The next few years will show whether that message has landed."

Thank you, Rachel, for giving me some of your time.

"You are most welcome. I think I will walk along this beach now, as it's one of my favourites."

NOTE: Few young people today know Rachel Carson's name. Yet, her influence still affects contemporary environmental policies and movements. She opened the world's eyes to the fragility of our ecosystems and the need for environmental stewardship.

To be more specific, Silent Spring, published in 1962, had multiple interconnected forces such as awareness of pesticides, the interconnectedness of ecosystems, scientific advocacy, legislative change, inspiration for activism, and causing a cultural Shift.

Rachel's Silent Spring is often credited with launching the contemporary environmental movement, making it a landmark publication in the fight for ecological awareness and protection.

For a detailed and well-informed biography, read On a Farther Shore--The Life and Legend of Rachel Carson, by William Souder, Crown Publishers, 2012.

HEDY LAMARR

1914–2001

Austrian American actress and inventor known for her beauty and contributions to technology. She co-invented frequency-hopping spread spectrum technology that laid the groundwork for modern wireless communication. Lamarr's dual career in Hollywood and scientific innovation challenged stereotypes in both fields.

"Any girl can be glamorous. All you have to do is stand still and look stupid."

Hedy Lamarr

HEDY LAMARR

Today, I am honoured to talk to a woman of extraordinary talent and resilience. Hedy Lamarr's life story is about her unwavering strength when faced with resistance. We're meeting in a small café, a peaceful retreat from the usual bustle of Los Angeles in the 1980s. The quiet ambience is a perfect setting for our conversation. Looking up from my table, I see Hedy striding vigorously towards me.

Now in her 70s, Hedy's appearance still echoes her glamorous self of the 1930s. Then, she was famous for her youthful and radiant look, with large, expressive eyes, full lips, and elegant features. She was often adorned in glamorous, high-fashion gowns to showcase her classic Hollywood allure. Now, her once smooth and youthful complexion has given way to natural signs of ageing, including gentle grey locks. At the peak of her Hollywood fame, a lush jet-black mane of hair accentuated her exotic looks, adding to her screen presence. She glides to a halt and takes the chair opposite me.

Heddy, I'm so glad you could make it today and that you agreed to discuss your fantastic life.

"I'm delighted to be here. These days, not many people know the Hedy Lamarr you've asked to meet. Where would you like to start?"

Well, let's at least start with that controversial 1933 film Ecstasy. I'm sure you must still have some strong views about that time.

"Ecstasy, yes! Can I ever forget it? It's one of my earliest films and one I'm most proud of. You probably know I appeared in a few innocent nude scenes that got many people all riled up. It was a disgrace, some critics said! Yet those discreet shots of me without clothes were harmless - absolutely nothing to get excited about."

Yes, amongst film enthusiasts, that film is still talked about today.

"The controversy surrounding it was significant and affected my career. But I didn't let it define me. I continued to work hard and prove my talent, and that's what I want to be remembered for. It certainly got me noticed, though, and indirectly found my first husband! I'll tell you about that later."

OK. Let's talk about your early life in Vienna before you went to Czechoslovakia to make that film and before Hollywood came calling.

"Right, then, let's go back to the very beginning. I was born in Vienna in 1914 in our family apartment in lovely, romantic, exquisite Vienna. Although we lived in a working-class neighbourhood, my family was affluent and cultured—my father was a banker, and my mother was a talented pianist. Between them, I had a well-rounded upbringing.

What did that mean in practice, Hedy Lemarr? Can you explain a bit further?

"Oh, do please call me Hedy. It's so much simpler! Anyway, I fell in love with the stage as a teenager and kept trying to act. Practising, practising, practising. I copied my mother. I copied how she walked and talked and her mannerisms and facial expressions. I copied the guests who came to our house. I copied people I saw on the street and the servants. I was a living copybook.

My father taught me that I must make my own decisions and think my own thoughts. When I was 15, I met the director and impresario Max Reinhardt, and he encouraged me to hold fast to my dream and that if I did, it would come true."

It seems Hedy that you held fast, and it did.

"Well, one day, I took a chance and slipped into the leading film studio in Vienna and asked them for a job. They were amused at this pushy teenager demanding to be employed and offered me a small script girl job at $5 an hour. Once there, I noticed a small extra part up for grabs and asked if I could have it. To my surprise, they gave it to me right away. That's how my film career began at sixteen!"

So, how did Ecstasy happen along?

"Berlin was then the centre of filmmaking. It wasn't that far away, so I took a chance and went there to look for work. That was when I was offered my first starring role in the Czech production called Ecstasy, scheduled for 1932. It was my first big opportunity, and I was like a cat with the hots. I was so excited.

Yes, amongst film enthusiasts, that film is still talked about today.

"The controversy surrounding it was significant and affected my career. But I didn't let it define me. I continued to work hard and prove my talent, and that's what I want to be remembered for. People focused more on the scandal than my talent. However, it did help in several ways.

Back in Vienna, I was offered a leading role in a stage play that caught Fritz Mandl's eye. He was the third richest man in Austria, having made his money in the armaments trade. Fritz laid siege to me with notes, flowers, dinner invitations and many presents. At first, I wasn't interested, and my disdain made him more determined.

Gradually, despite my resistance, I got to know him and found there was nothing he didn't know. He had a fantastic brain. Soon, I was madly in love with him, and we married once I left the stage show. However, at 19, I soon discovered that I was locked into a prison of gold and was no longer an individual. I was defined by being the wife of Fritz Mandl."

How depressing. How on earth did you escape from that prison?

"It wasn't easy. Mandl was an insecure and jealous man who even had his servants watch over me. He was afraid his trophy wife would try to go back to the stage. But then my father died, and I changed completely. While my father was alive, I tolerated a lousy marriage for his sake. Now I knew I must run away and make plans to go to Hollywood. It's a long story, but in 1937, there were newspaper headlines: Ecstasy star to quit rich mate for the stage."

I'm on the edge of my seat here, Hedy! Before I die of frustration, please say how you got away.

"It was dramatic. No motion picture could have made it more exciting. I left Vienna that night, veiled and incognito and clutching all my worldly possessions. I went straight to London. I didn't even wait for one of those quickie divorces that were so popular then."

What happened when you arrived in London?

"You may not believe this, but at a small dinner party, I met Louis B. Mayer, head of MGM, who happened to be in town to inspect some studios. After some discussions, he offered me a minimal contract if I paid my own fare to America."

Typical mean Mayer. Still, was that it--were you then on your way to stardom, Hedy?

"Not quite. I rejected his miserable offer and walked out. I wanted better terms and bought a ticket on the Normandie, one the largest ships in the world. When she sailed, I was on board, and so were the Mayers, and we became friendly. I attracted a lot of male attention on board and paraded them past Mr Mayer! That did the trick, and he upped my offer depending on me taking English lessons and changing my name."

So that is how you became Hedy Lamarr?

"Yes, Hedwig Kiesler was my birth name. Louis B. Mayer wanted something more glamorous, more suited to the Hollywood image. Hedy came from my first name, and "Lamarr" was a tribute to Barbara La Marr, a silent film actress who had passed away in the 1920s."

Can you explain what caused your rise to stardom once established in Hollywood?

"Again, I was lucky. First, the renowned Max Reinhardt I mentioned, who had encouraged me when I was just 15, was directing a play in Vienna. There were lots of newspaper journalists watching, and suddenly, he turned to the reporters and announced in a loud voice that everybody present could hear: "Hedy Kiesler is the most beautiful girl in the world."

Instantly, the reporters scribbled it down, and it appeared in other newspapers, capitals, countries, and continents. Later, Mayer took up the description and used it for publicity, claiming to have invented it!

My first contract was my second lucky break in Hollywood. It was opposite Charles Boyer, the leading romantic man in American films. This film caught the attention of Hollywood directors and audiences alike. Next came roles opposite Clark Gable, Spencer Tracy, Judy Garland and others; I guess you could say I was much in demand."

All this film success, and at the same time, you worked on your scientific inventions. How on earth did you manage that? Being a star could hardly have left you a lot of spare time. How did you balance your love for acting with your passion for science and invention?

"You're right. It wasn't always easy to find that balance. But I needed that intellectual stimulation. Acting was my career, but seldom challenged me in the way I craved. I was often typecast as the exotic, beautiful woman, and after a while, it became frustrating. Meanwhile, behind the scenes, I constantly tinkered with ideas and created things. My mind needed to stay active, and science gave me that outlet."

You invented frequency-hopping technology, which is a massive contribution and an essential part of communication systems. How did that come about?

"I was always curious, and during my first marriage to Fritz Mandl in Vienna, we had lots of dinners and social occasions when invited experts talked about new technologies and weaponry. I listened in and gained a great deal of secret knowledge. Later, during World War

II, when I became upset at the loss of life from our failing torpedoes, I decided to help the Allied war effort. I pursued my interest in radio technology and how it guided torpedoes to their target. At that time, they used an expanding wire to tell the torpedo to adjust its course."

You thought you could improve on that?

"It seemed worth a try. The enemy easily jammed radio signals. So, I developed the basic principle that constantly switching frequencies would make the signal harder to detect or jam."

Did you work on this brainwave alone?

"No, I collaborated with a brilliant music composer called George Antheil. He was what you might call a Renaissance Man, multi-talented and seemingly able to do anything. For example, he was once a government inspector of munitions. He also pioneered the synchronisation of numerous mechanical pianolas that used paper scrolls punched with holes to create the notes. He produced fantastic music. George helped me figure out how to link the frequency changes between the transmitter and receiver on a torpedo using a mechanism similar to the ones he used in player pianos."

Some people have seen you, too, Hedy, as a Renaissance Woman, a film star, and a producer of inventions. How did your frequency-hopping idea go down with the armed services?

"We submitted the patented idea to the U.S. Navy in 1942, but they didn't take it seriously. Only much later did the technology become valuable for other things."

Yes, Bluetooth, Wi-Fi and GPS all depend on your invention. You could potentially have made a fortune.

"If only. But that's another story about why George and I lost out financially."

That must have been frustrating. Do you think being a woman—and a

Hollywood actress at that - had something to do with it?

"Absolutely. Back then, no one expected a woman, let alone an actress, to develop something so technical. The Navy found it hard to reconcile their glamorous image of me with the fact that I had a serious interest in science and innovation. It was incredibly limiting, but I didn't let it stop me. I kept inventing, even if recognition came much later."

Although your work wasn't fully appreciated then, you're often credited as one of the pioneers of modern communication technology.

"It's bittersweet. It's wonderful that my ideas have contributed to the technology people now use daily. As I complained back then, there was never even a letter, never a thank you, and never any money. But, in the end, my work's impact is more important."

Speaking of personal struggles, your life off-screen has seemed as eventful as your professional one. You were married six times. How did these marriages affect your career and your personal growth?

Putting down her coffee cup somewhat abruptly: "Oh, my marriages... well, they were chapters in my life story. Each marriage was different, and not all were happy, but they shaped me differently."

How exactly did those relationships impact you?

"Each marriage had its ups and downs. My work and need for independence always got in the way. Even today, it's hard for men to accept a woman who is both strong-willed and successful. My later marriages were brief, and I became somewhat disillusioned with them. They never seemed to work out as I'd hoped.

Did those relationships distract you from your work or give you a kind of stability?

"They were a distraction, but I wouldn't say they derailed my career. If anything, they gave me life experience, both good and bad. I drew from them as an actress and an inventor. The emotional rollercoaster of those relationships certainly added depth to my work. But I won't lie; they could be exhausting. It was never easy trying to balance my personal and professional life."

Looking back, do you regret any of your six marriages?

"No, I don't believe in regret. Each of those men taught me something, whether about myself or the world. And while none were perfect for me, they all shaped who I became. I think, though, that I would have been better off if I'd focused more on my interests and less on trying to please the men in my life."

That's a powerful reflection. You've lived such a dynamic life filled with both triumphs and challenges. What do you think was the most difficult part of being a star and an inventor?

"The hardest part was being taken seriously. As I said earlier, people had a very narrow view of me. They saw the glamorous movie star and assumed that was all there was. But I was much more than that, and it was frustrating to feel like I had to prove myself constantly."

Do you feel like your beauty was both a blessing and a curse?

"Absolutely. My looks opened doors for me in Hollywood, but they also put me in a box. People were so focused on my face that they didn't see what was behind it. It's flattering to be considered beautiful, but after a while, it becomes limiting. You want to be appreciated for more than just for your appearance. That's partly why I turned to inventing. It allowed me to express a different side of myself."

What would you say to the women of today, whether in acting or pursuing careers in science or technology?

"I'd tell them never to let anyone put you in a box. If you have more than one passion, pursue them all. Don't let society's expectations limit you. And most importantly, don't wait for recognition. Keep pushing forward and creating because your work and ideas will ultimately matter."

That's excellent advice. One final question. When you reflect on your life, what are you most proud of?

"I'm proud that I didn't let the world define me. I wasn't just an actress or just a wife. I was an inventor, a thinker, and a dreamer. And while I don't feel fully appreciated, I know I left a mark on the world, both on-screen and off. That's enough for me."

Thank you so much, Hedy. It's been an absolute pleasure speaking with you today.

"It's been lovely revisiting these memories with you. If you'll excuse me, I'll get back to working on my new kind of traffic light and finalising some proposed improvements to the aerodynamics and noise reduction of the supersonic Concorde airliner. Thanks for the coffee!"

With that startling announcement, this once "the most beautiful woman in the world", perhaps still one of the most intriguing, was gone.

NOTE: The 82-year-old Hedy Lamar was awarded the Electronic Frontier Foundation's Pioneer Award in 1997 and, at 85, died peacefully in her sleep. Had Lamarr and her co-inventor Antheil received royalties or compensation based on the modern usage of her invention, its value would now be worth billions of dollars. However, since their patent was not commercially utilised in their lifetime, they did not personally benefit from its financial success. She was also known to have worked on a noise reduction idea for Concord in her final years.

For a fuller account of this remarkable woman and her gripping story, you can do no better than read Hedy's Folly, by Richard Rhodes, Doubleday 2011.

RUTH BADER GINSBURG

1933–2020

Ruth Bader Ginsburg was an American Supreme Court Justice and trailblazing advocate for gender equality and civil rights. Her legal career, marked by her fight against gender discrimination, transformed U.S. law. Her legacy and belief that the law must adapt and reflect real needs endures.

"Fight for the things that you care about, but do it in a way that will lead others to join you,"

Ginsburgh, at the Radcliffe Institute 2015

RUTH BADER GINSBURG

We're meeting in the hallowed halls of the US Supreme Court, where Ginsburg has presided for 25 years, from her appointment in 1993. I am keen to meet this most revered justice and have considered carefully what I want to ask her. Much of Ginsburg's life is well documented, so I'll ask about some of its lesser-known aspects. Today, she's wearing one of her famous, dark, sophisticated blouses complemented by her iconic lace ruff. I note pearl earrings and stylish handbag, a touch of personal flair that reflects her strong character and dedication to her work.

Justice Ginsburg, your work as a champion for gender equality and civil rights is well known. I'd like to start our conversation by exploring some of your personal and less-documented aspects. Is that alright?

"Let's see how we go. If your questions are too intrusive, I'll tell you immediately."

You've read widely and have a broad interest in the arts. Can I ask if there's a book, some music, or a piece of art you treasure the most or that has had the most profound influence on your life outside of the law?

"That's an interesting question because my life is mostly about the law. But beyond that sphere, opera has profoundly influenced me, mainly Mozart. His Marriage of Figaro constantly stimulates me, and its portrayal of human emotions seems timeless. It's witty and touching, and it reminds me that while power struggles are real, love and intellect can prevail in the end. Mozart helps me stay calm during the most challenging cases."

So, has music always played a big part in your life?

"Yes. While I could play the piano as a child, I have always enjoyed music as a listener, not a performer. Music is a significant part of my identity, and I often find solace and inspiration. It is also a source of relaxation and a catalyst for my work in advocacy."

What about personal struggles? You're a tireless advocate for gender equality. Have there been moments when you wondered whether the fight was worth it? How did you push through?

"There were many moments of doubt, particularly early in my career. One of the worst times was after graduating from law school. I couldn't land a job."

That's always puzzled me, Justice Ginsburg. With impeccable credentials and a first in your class at Columbia Law Review, it seems scandalous that no law firm in New York wanted to hire you. Was it that bad?

"It was that bad then, mainly due to male resistance. Being a woman, married, and bringing up a child made me unemployable. It was frustrating and made me wonder whether the system could change. Yet I kept pushing since I sincerely believed in the principles I was fighting for. Like all starting-out lawyers, I did my share of clerking, which taught me a lot."

So, what did you do when you couldn't find a decent job?

"I was approached to work in Sweden for a couple of years. So off I went, complete with my family. I helped to write a legal text on comparative law, though not many people around here know that. They'd probably be surprised that I speak quite a bit of Swedish."

What kept you going, pushing for what you want?

"I kept reminding myself that change doesn't happen overnight. On a personal level, my husband, Marty, was wonderful in keeping me going. He had an unwavering belief in me that was infectious. He always cheered me up by reminding me that the setbacks weren't the end, just detours. I called him my "Constant Uplifter.""

He also took on a lot of the household chores, I believe?

"Yes, my culinary efforts were a disaster, and Marty, thank goodness, became the family cook. He also taught me to laugh at myself, which was one of the most valuable life lessons. Marty was also blessed with a beautiful sense of humour. He reminded me not to take life too seriously. People might not realise how much humour played a part in our marriage and helped with my ability to navigate high-pressure situations.

The kind of law I practice can be intense and all-consuming. Marty's humour encouraged me to step back and find a balance. Sometimes, it was just him cracking a joke at dinner after a long day to remind me there's a world outside the courtroom. He was the only guy I ever dated who cared whether I had a brain. He was just so damn smart."

Let's briefly examine your marriage more closely as it sheds valuable light on your professional career. Your parents-in-law realised they had gained an older daughter with far more ambition and determination than suggested by your glamour.

"Yes, they treated me so well. My father-in-law, by the way, was the best person I had ever danced with! My mother-in-law took me aside on my wedding day and put a pair of earplugs in my hands. She explained that the secret of a happy marriage was: "It helps sometimes to be a little deaf. "She even gave me a set of golf clubs, which shows you her priorities! As for our marriage, we were determined to share careers, though we were unsure how. I didn't fancy medicine, which was one possibility, and it came down to Harvard Law School, and Marty followed my lead."

Marty's extraordinary enthusiasm for dual careers suggests he was a man ahead of his time, surely?

"I think it stemmed from his enormous self-confidence that allowed him to see life as full of possibilities rather than a set of gender norms.

I had great faith in his judgement, and when I crashed the car one day, Marty announced that from now on, he'd be my chauffeur. He also worked incredibly hard, and I wasn't surprised when he emerged as a world-class tax expert in his law firm."

Apart from your marriage, can I ask if there was a surprising relationship you built over the years that others might not have expected?

"Without a doubt, my lasting relationship with Nino, Justice Antonin Scalia. He was a long-serving member of the Supreme Court. Many people know we were friends despite our ideological differences yet may not grasp the depth of our friendship."

Can you explain that a bit more, Justice Ginsburg?

"Nino and I saw the law differently, yet we respected each other immensely. We had much in common, such as our formative years in Manhattan, ethnic investment in family, and love of opera. These formed the anchors of our friendship. Together, we shared a respect for the craft of argument. Nino sharpened my thinking, and I like to believe I sharpened his. Nino often pushed me to clarify my reasoning, and I think I did the same for him. Our debates were fierce but respectful, and I valued him greatly for that."

It must have been interesting to work so closely with someone who disagreed with you on so much. Is there one case in mind where you felt an emotional reaction but had to set it aside for objective reasoning?

"That's a tricky question because, as justices, we train to separate our emotions from the law. But of course, we're human, and sometimes that isn't easy. One particular case that comes to mind is Ledbetter v. Goodyear Tire & Rubber Co., which dealt with gender pay discrimination.

Lilly Ledbetter's story mirrored the discrimination many women experience, which is why the case impacted me. But the written law was not on her side, and we had to follow the statute. In that case, my belief drove my written Dissent to suggest that the law was wrong. I wasn't emotional in the sense of being irrational. However, I allowed my passion for fairness and equality to surface in my writing. Eventually, that original Dissent led to a change in the law signed by President Obama in 2009. So, in that case, emotion and reason worked in harmony."

You mentioned writing; your Dissents are legendary. I'm curious if a particular personal ritual or habit helped you maintain such clarity when writing or thinking through these complex legal issues.

"Writing, for me, is both a method of communication and a means of clarifying my thinking. Whenever I feel stuck, I take a walk. That is my ritual. There's something about the rhythm of walking that frees the mind. When wrestling with a particularly knotty legal issue, I often go outside and let my thoughts roam freely. When I return, I usually have a clear sense of direction.

Also, I always try to write for a broad audience. I don't want my opinions or dissents filled with legal jargon that only lawyers can understand. If a decision affects people's lives, they deserve to know why we ruled the way we did."

In your dissents and opinions, you often challenged societal norms. Outside the legal world, is there any one person who has inspired your thinking or approach to justice?

"There is one who had a profound influence on me, Eleanor Roosevelt, the president's wife. She had a massive sense of responsibility to the world and was fearless in her advocacy for human rights. I admired how she balanced her struggles with her public role. Her work with the United Nations on human rights was particularly inspiring because it showed how a person can have a global influence. She had a keen sense of justice. Like her, I believe justice is a national and international concern."

Your advocacy and arguments for justice have undoubtedly achieved a global reach. If you could glimpse fifty years into the future of U.S. law, what would you hope or fear to see?

"That we will continue to expand and protect civil rights for all people, regardless of gender, race, sexual orientation, or any other characteristic that might divide us. I hope to see a future where the rights we've fought for are preserved and strengthened. We may see a regression, and reactionary forces could erode hard-won gains. But I believe in the resilience of our system and have faith in future generations. If there's one thing I've learned from my time on the bench, it's that progress is slow but relentless.

That's most encouraging. Many people know you as a model of dedication. I particularly want to understand how you handle burnout or fatigue, especially during difficult work moments.

"Ah, burnout, that's real, even for Supreme Court Justices. One thing I've always tried to do is compartmentalise. When I am at work, I give it my full attention. But when I am with my family or at the opera, I force myself to step away from the law entirely. As I've mentioned, opera plays a considerable part in my ability to recharge.

I also maintain a rigorous exercise routine. I've done so all my life. As a teenager, I loved riding, skiing and water skiing. Even after my cancer treatments, I have been working out with my trainer, Bryant Johnson. I have built rigorous exercise into my daily life, which includes strength training and yoga. My workouts are not just about physical health; they also deliberately reflect my determination and resilience. Physical exercise has helped me maintain the stamina necessary to do the intense intellectual work required by the Court."

Yes, your dedication to exercise has been a source of inspiration for many people. It highlights your belief in caring for one's body and

mind, regardless of age. It contributes to your image and why you are often affectionately called The Notorious RBG.

"I never liked that sort of pretentious labelling. Next question!"

Again, can we touch on humour? Was there ever a time when a well-placed joke or moment of humour made a difference in a high-pressure situation?

"Oh, absolutely! One moment from my early years on the bench comes to mind. We were dealing with a particularly contentious case, and there was real tension in the room. My fellow Justice, Sandra Day O'Connor, had this wonderful, understated sense of humour. Despite the seriousness of the occasion, Sandra made a sly comment about the absurdity of arguing over something so small, given the more significant stakes at play. Her timing was impeccable, and it immediately broke the tension. We all laughed, and it shifted the tone of the conversation. Humour is essential in those moments because it reminds us not to take ourselves too seriously, even when the issues we're dealing with are severe."

As the first woman on the Court, did Justice O'Connor mentor you in any way? What's something she taught you of particular value, something that might not be obvious?

"Sandra and I shared a deep bond, though she was the senior justice. One thing she impressed upon me early on was the importance of patience. She had a very pragmatic approach to the law, often reminding me that sometimes, incremental change is more effective than sweeping decisions. In my early years, I was more idealistic, wanting immediate changes. But Sandra's wisdom showed me the value of gradual progress. She used to say, "Ruth, the law is like a garden - you plant the seeds, but it takes time for them to grow."

Something that you seldom mention is being Jewish and what that meant to you as you grew up. Would you mind talking about that

briefly?

"Well, alright. But it does indeed have to be brief. You see, while I honour my heritage, its ethical teachings and values, I stopped being a religious jew around the time my mother died. Our local synagogue behaved towards my father in a way I'd rather not discuss now. It had a terrible impact, and I eventually became a non-practising jew."

Thank you for sharing that with me. Finally, my last question is: What would you say to advise a young judge starting today?

"Always remember that your role is to interpret the law impartially, not based on personal preferences or society pressures. Be patient; don't be afraid to write dissenting opinions when you feel the majority is wrong. Also, never forget that lawmaking institutions can and should engage in dialogue about repairing our fragile and perilous world.

I'd stress to that young judge that their formal Dissent can plant seeds that may eventually grow into the law of the land. Also, recognise that the law, like society, evolves. So, remain open to learning and adapting as new challenges emerge. Most of all, I'd urge a new judge to protect their independence fiercely and ensure their decisions are grounded in fairness and justice, not short-term political gains."

That's excellent advice, Justice Ginsburg. Thank you so much for sharing these personal insights.

"It's been a thoughtful experience, and I've enjoyed it. Perhaps not on a par with opera, but even so, most worthwhile!"

NOTE: Ruth Bader Ginsburg died in 2020, leaving an enormous legacy. In the short term, her trailblazing litigation strategy transformed the legal landscape of gender equality. Her work helped break down barriers for women and marginalised groups.

In the long term, her impact extends far beyond individual cases. She inspired generations of women and men to fight for equality. Her ability to influence legal thought, even in legendary court Dissents, and her emphasis on incremental change while keeping an eye on long-term goals will shape the legal world for decades. More importantly, her vision of a more equal and just society has left an indelible mark, encouraging future generations to continue her work of expanding rights for all.

Jane Sherron De Hart's biography of Ginsburg, A Life, is a comprehensive and absorbing achievement. It covers many demanding legal cases, not all directly connected to Ginsburg, but it is well worth reading.

To get closer to this remarkable woman, check out My Own Words by Ruth Bader Ginsburg, Simon & Schuster 2016.

Also, check out the excellent film of Ginsburg's early years: On the Basis of Sex, written by her real-life nephew and starring Felicity Jones as Ginsburg.

ZAHA HADID

1950-2016

Hadid is an Iraqi-British architect known for her groundbreaking and futuristic designs. The first woman to receive the Pritzker Architecture Prize, her work includes iconic buildings like the Guangzhou Opera House and the London Aquatics Centre. Hadid's visionary approach of using painting as a design tool to reshape contemporary architecture continues to inspire future generations.

"There are 360 degrees, so why stick to one?"

Zaha Hadid: The Complete Works by Zaha Hadid, 2015

ZAHA HADID

Opposite me, there's an empty modernist chair. This attractive piece of furniture discretely echoes Hadid's famed architectural style. It's almost sculptural, with sleek lines, blending art and functionality. Neither is the space around me empty; many architectural sketches, 3D models, and design books are scattered with care across the room.

Once described by the Guardian as the "Queen of Curves," Zaha bustles in, wrapped in her trademark black cloak, her lustrous hair overflowing onto her shoulders. After shaking my hand, she sits in the empty chair smiling; her direct look suggests she's curious or perhaps wary about the conversation.

"Well then, how can I help you today?"

First, thank you for agreeing to see me here in your London Practice. I have many questions, but can I start with one memorable comment you have made: "There are 360 degrees, so why stick to one?" I love that question, Ms Hadid, as it seems to have driven your entire career.

"You're correct. But please call me Zaha. You see, I didn't enter architecture to create the same buildings over and over again. I've never been attracted to repeating formulas. For me, architecture is all about exploration. Why limit yourself? The world is filled with many possibilities, so why not use all the available tools?"

Can you clarify this last point about available tools so I can better understand what you mean?

"Whether it's new materials, digital technology or even mathematics, architecture has the power to shape how we experience the world and how we live and move within it."

So, are these tools transformative?

"Absolutely. Early in my career, when I started designing conceptual buildings, people would look at my sketches and say they were beautiful but impossible to build. But as technology evolved, we gained the means to turn those sketches into reality. For example, digital modelling allows for forms that would have been unthinkable decades ago. It's opened up so many new possibilities, and that's exciting to me. The Heydar Aliyev Centre in Azerbaijan, the Guangzhou Opera House in Southern China, and the Aquatics Centre in London are these projects that became possible through digital innovation."

Looking back at those projects, especially the ones that seemed impossible at the time, do you ever think about your role as a pioneer, particularly as a woman in such a male-dominated field?

Zaha shrugs slightly: "I never set out to be known as a female architect! The focus has always been on the work, not my gender. But yes, of course, it hasn't been easy. You make lots of sacrifices to get where you want. You probably know that the architectural world can be challenging for women, especially in leadership roles. Still, I've never accepted that as a reason to limit myself. If anything, it's fuelled me to push harder.

I'm also proud to have been able to break through those barriers and show there's room for women at the absolute top of this field. But ultimately, it's not about being a woman; it's about doing the work. The work is what matters."

You've inspired a whole new generation of architects to think differently about design. With each project, it seems you're redefining what architecture can be. And you have done so much. Have you ever considered how far you've come since those early days in Baghdad?

Impatiently, Zaha shakes her head: "I don't think about it much. Architecture is about the future, about what comes next. I don't dwell on the past. But of course, Baghdad shaped me, growing up in the 1950s and 60s. It was a time of incredible optimism and so much ambition. New buildings, new cities, that spirit of invention, of looking forward, has stayed with me."

I accept that you don't dwell on the past, but I really want to learn more about how that little girl in Iraq became one of the world's most admired architects.

"OK, I'll try! I was born in Baghdad in 1950 to an upper-class family. My father was a leading politician in the 1930s and 40s, and my mother was an artist from Mosul. Let me tell you how I got interested in architecture. Well, in those days, we went on many childhood trips to the ancient Sumerian cities in Southern Iraq, and that experience sparked my interest. As I was good at maths, I studied it at the American University of Beirut and moved to London in 1972 to study Architecture."

Coming to London to study must have been a turning point. How did it affect your approach?

"It was undoubtedly freeing. I wasn't bound by the rules or traditions defining architecture at the Architectural Association, and I had fantastic mentors. They didn't just feed me the answers; they encouraged me to explore and experiment."

Can you give me a real example of that happening?

"I remember working on "The Peak," a conceptual design for a leisure club in Hong Kong in 1983. I didn't care if it was practical. I wanted to explore movement and fragmentation and architecture as an extension of the landscape. It was a bold idea, and many people thought I was crazy."

Still, if I'm correct, it was never actually built. That seems to have been a common reaction to your early work.

"Constantly. Even the most supportive clients often failed to see how we could translate those ideas into reality. Many of my projects were rejected, or they remained unbuilt. Instead, for years, I was more known for my paintings and drawings rather than buildings. Not only was the Peak not built, but my plan for an opera house in Cardiff was chosen as the best by the competition jury, but the funding body refused to pay for it, and the work went to a less ambitious architect."

That must have been so depressing. What was your response to such news?

Zaha chuckles: "I asked them: do you want nothing but mediocrity!" You see, I'm not interested in playing it safe. Architecture needs to challenge you. It needs to make you question your surroundings."

Then, in the early 90s, you finally started turning those radical ideas into built form. The Vitra Fire Station in Germany was the launching pad of your architectural career, right?

Yes, you're well-informed. Vitra was significant because it was the first of my larger commissions to be built. The design was about movement, about the building becoming part of the environment rather than standing in isolation. I wanted to convey a sense of fluidity and energy, which I've always been drawn to. I didn't want a typical box-like structure. Even though it was a fire station, a place that's supposed to be static until an emergency happens, it had to reflect the idea of constant motion."

I recognise that ethos. Creating movement through space is so much part of your work. Another stunning example is The Heydar Aliyev Centre, which you've just completed in Baku, Azerbaijan. Can you perhaps talk a bit about this extraordinary place?

"I wanted a fluid form that emerges by using the landscape's natural topography and encompassing how the individual parts of the Centre fit together. For example, the Centre's functions, including its many entrances, appear as part of a single continuous surface. This flowing form was an opportunity to connect the various cultural spaces while guaranteeing each element of the Centre can have its own identity and privacy. As it folds inside, the skin erodes to become an element of the interior landscape of the Centre."

The building almost flows into its surroundings. Was that your original vision for that project?

"Exactly. With the Heydar Aliyev Centre, I wanted a space that feels alive. Architecture, to me, is not just about making a functional structure. It's about creating an experience, something immersive. The building had to be fluid and organic. Baku is a city with a rich history, but it's also looking toward the future. I wanted the building to feel like it was emerging from the ground, like a wave or a piece of fabric unfurling. It's almost like a landscape in itself. Why restrict us to rectangles and squares when the world around us is filled with curves, with fluid forms?"

The fluidity you often talk about seems so intangible and futuristic. Your buildings don't seem bound by traditional time or geometry. One of the most interesting to me is the Bergisel Ski Jump in Austria. You turned what was a pedestrian concept into a futuristic marvel.

"Yes, but I had a real fight on my hands. I battled not only the traditionalists but also against time. I created "an organic hybrid", a cross between a tower and a bridge. Its form gives a sense of movement and speed. It had to be completed within one year before the next international competition. Just after it opened, Austrian ski jumper Thomas Morgenstern broke a world record there, soaring an impressive distance of 143.5 meters."

Yes, it was a thrilling moment that showcased his prowess and your jump's cutting-edge design, which optimised aerodynamics and visibility. You've also often talked about your fascination with abstraction and modern art. Artists like Malevich, Lissitzky, and the Suprematists movement seem to have significantly affected you.

"I saw them as going beyond painting colours on a canvas. What excited me was that they were imagining new worlds and new ways of seeing space. Their work significantly influenced modern art, including my own, by emphasising abstraction and geometric forms. Their focus challenged conventional perceptions of art and opened new avenues for artistic exploration, especially in architecture. For me, architecture must reach beyond functionality, such as merely creating shelter. Like Malevich's paintings, my buildings explore space, movement, and form. The idea is always to disrupt the conventional ways of thinking about buildings."

Your disruptions have often attracted much criticism over the years - whether it's the complexity of your designs or the cost of your projects. How have you dealt with that?

"I've always found it amusing. Of course, people will criticise what they don't understand. But architecture shouldn't just come down to function and budget. It's an art form; like any art, it provokes different reactions. My work has been called extravagant or impractical. But I believe good architecture should challenge and elevate people's experience of space."

Do you see your legacy as being about more than just the buildings you've created?

"Architecture is constantly evolving. What's important is that we keep pushing the boundaries and experimenting. If my work has opened doors for other architects to think differently and to be more daring, then that's a legacy I can be proud of. I want people to understand that architecture isn't static - it's alive, it's dynamic. We shouldn't be afraid to take risks, to fail even. That's how progress happens."

You've consistently stayed on the cutting edge. Your work challenges, inspires and pushes boundaries. I imagine we'll be talking about your influence for generations to come.

She smiles faintly: Who knows? I hope so. But as I said earlier, I don't think much about what's behind me. I'm always looking forward. There's still so much left to explore.

Finally, you've never positively used the issue of being a woman architect. Is there a particular reason for avoiding it?

"I'm not avoiding it. I don't mind if it helps younger people know they can break through the glass ceiling. But I admit that I have never felt part of the male-dominant architectural establishment. As a woman, you're always an outsider. That's OK. I like being on the edge."

I have no doubt you'll keep showing us the way. Thank you for spending this time with me.

"Not at all. I've enjoyed this chance to talk about what I love."

NOTE: This conversation is entirely fictional, an imagined exchange based on Zaha Hadid's public persona and known viewpoints. Though Zaha Hadid passed away in 2016, her influence continues to resonate throughout architecture. She completed over 950 projects throughout her career, with approximately 500 visible and in use today. Recognised by Forbes in 2013 as one of the World's Most Powerful Women, Hadid became the first woman to win the prestigious Pritzker Architecture Prize in 2004, which honours those whose work demonstrates vision and commitment to the built environment. In 2012, she was made a Dame Commander of the Order of the British Empire, and in 2014, she received an honorary degree from Goldsmiths for her bold and inventive approach to architecture.

Hadid redefined the very language of architecture, leaving a lasting imprint on cities and landscapes across the globe. Our imaginary conversation wasn't just about architecture but also about innovation, ambition, and the courage to challenge convention. Zaha Hadid's legacy will continue to inspire, and her bold vision will shape the future of design for decades to come.

No comprehensive biographies have been published, though one or more are underway. The heavily illustrated book "Zaha Hadid" by Philip Jodidio, published by Taschen, presents many of her seminal buildings.

For more information on Hadid, see:

Britannica entry: https://www.britannica.com/biography/Zaha-Hadid

From Zaha Hadid Foundation: "The Zaha Hadid Foundation is dedicated to the work and artistic legacy of Zaha Hadid, to the advancement of research and education in areas pertaining to both, and to areas in architecture, design, and related disciplines that reflect her creative spirit." see https://www.zhfoundation.com/

NOTE 1: HAVE A HELPFUL CHAT WITH THE GREATS

Imagine sitting with Socrates over coffee or engaging in a lively debate about the power of words with Maya Angelou. These dialogues with the greats are not just imaginative conversations with historical figures. They're thrilling opportunities to explore their ideas and philosophies and experience navigating their world. The prospect of such encounters can pique your interest, keep you intrigued, and stimulate you in so many ways. There are numerous instances of people having imaginary dialogues with historical figures.

- Jeremy Taylor's The Dialogue of the Dead was first published in 1682. The work is a philosophical dialogue that explores themes of life, death, and the afterlife through a fictional conversation between two deceased characters. This exploration is not just intriguing; it's intellectually stimulating.

- In Conversations with the Dead' by William L. DeAndrea, an American mystery writer, a detective engages in discussions with the deceased to solve crimes. This unique blend of mystery and philosophical musings will keep you engaged and intrigued.

- Plato's "The Last Days of Socrates," while primarily a philosophical text, features dialogues between Socrates and his friends about morality, justice, and the afterlife. Plato's Socratic dialogues occur with historical figures like Glaucon and Thrasymachus, exploring ethics and knowledge.

- "The Book of Dead Philosophers" by English philosopher Simon Critchley explores various philosophers' lives and thoughts by imagining conversations that reflect their ideas on life and death.

- "The New Atlantis" by Francis Bacon imagines a dialogue with the ideal society, reflecting Bacon's views on science and enlightenment.

- Timothy Ferriss, an American entrepreneur, investor, author, podcaster, and lifestyle guru, wrote "A Dialog on the Universe." The book imagines conversations with figures like Albert Einstein and Carl Sagan about the cosmos and human existence.

WHY BOTHER?

The benefits of conversations with dead or even fictional people include:

Intellectual Growth

Engaging with the thoughts of great thinkers can spark one's intellectual curiosity. When you "talk" with figures like Rachel Carson or Von Salomé, you might explore how they refused to let being female limit their horizons and ambitions. "Imagination is more important than knowledge," claimed Einstein, which is a strong argument for embracing creativity and challenging the conventional wisdom surrounding you today. Envisioning these dialogues pushes your mind to explore new ideas and think critically.

Cultural Awareness

Historical figures often reflect the cultures and societies of their time. Discussing ideas with the much-travelled Madam Tussaud or Marie Montessori can deepen understanding of identity and feminism. Through such discussions, you may appreciate the diverse perspectives that have shaped our and their worlds. Such interchanges can foster a sense of empathy toward different cultures and experiences.

Emotional Connection

Imagining a dialogue with a figure like Ruth Bader Ginsberg or Mary Seacole could evoke deep emotions. Their resilience and commitment can inspire us to reflect on our values. This emotional connection can motivate you to face your challenges, reminding you that perseverance is crucial, no matter the odds.

Moral and Ethical Reflection

When you engage with thinkers like Voltaire or Mary Wollstonecraft, you explore moral dilemmas and ethical questions. Their challenges can help you to consider the broader impact of your actions. Imagining a dialogue around these principles can help clarify your values and navigate complex ethical landscapes.

Inspiration and Motivation

History is filled with stories of triumph over adversity. Imagine a conversation with figures like Harriet Tubman, who helped free Southern slaves by the thousand, or Zaha Hadid, whose ideas were constantly rejected for years yet went on to build over 500 stunning buildings you can see today. These people and their dealing with setbacks and adversity can inspire you to pursue your dreams. The resulting dialogues can remind you that every incredible journey starts with a single step, perhaps fuelling your motivation to chase your aspirations.

Problem-Solving Skills

Imaginary discussions with innovators like the late Steve Jobs or the long-gone Henry Ford may help to enhance your problem-solving abilities. Jobs was known for his belief that "innovation distinguishes between a leader and a follower." Ford, who invented the production line, kept asking how to manufacture quicker, cheaper and better. Contemplating how such people approached a difficult challenge may offer fresh perspectives and innovative solutions. Such creative thinking is vital in today's fast-paced world.

Enhanced Communication Skills

Engaging with great past communicators can teach the art of persuasion and rhetoric. Their ability to convey powerful messages through words can be an invaluable presentation class. Reflecting on how such people express ideas can sharpen your communication skills. Marie Stopes, who launched the first birth control clinics, relentlessly presented her ideas through tireless lecturing, issuing books, pamphlets, and other ways to engage with people.

Historical Context

Imagined dialogues with past figures can help you better understand historical events and their contexts. Conversing with someone like Winston Churchill can provide insight into leadership during times of crisis. His famous quote, "Success is not final, failure is not fatal: It is the courage to continue that counts", can help focus on the importance of resilience in adversity. Understanding history through these conversations may enable you to appreciate the complexities of the past and inform your perspective on current events.

Personal Identity Exploration

Imaginary discussions can be a mirror for self-exploration. Engaging with someone like Virginia Woolf can prompt you to reflect on your identity and creativity. Woolf's belief that "for most of history, Anonymous was a woman" can lead you to consider your narrative in a broader context. Such dialogues encourage you to think critically about your place and how your experiences shape who you are.

Creative Inspiration

Finally, engaging with the greats can spark creativity. Talking with now-inaccessible artists like Picasso, writers like James Joyce, or musicians like Beethoven can inspire one's artistic side.

Conclusion

Dialogues with the greats may seem far-fetched or even frivolous. Yet they offer a treasure trove of benefits beyond mere entertainment. They stimulate intellectual curiosity, enhance emotional awareness, and encourage ethical reflection. Whether you're seeking inspiration, cultural insights, or creative bursts, these imaginative exchanges can profoundly impact your perspective on life.

As Franklin D. Roosevelt famously noted. "Embrace the wisdom of the past to shape your future!"

NOTE 2: REMEMBERING REMARKABLE WOMEN

We remember remarkable women in at least seven distinct but overlapping ways for their:

1. Historical Impact

Women who have significantly shaped history, politics, or social movements. Their actions or decisions resulted in long-lasting changes in governance, human rights, or public policy. Figures like Cleopatra, who influenced the fate of the Roman Empire, or Joan of Arc, who played a crucial role in France's national identity, would fall into this category.

2. Cultural or Artistic Influence

Women whose contributions to culture, literature, art, or science left a lasting mark continue to be influential long after their passing. For instance, Jane Austen and Frida Kahlo remain cultural icons whose creations still resonate with audiences and influence contemporary literature and art.

3. Pioneering Spirit

This involves women who broke barriers in traditionally male-dominated fields, setting the stage for future generations. Marie Curie (science) and Amelia Earhart (aviation) are examples of women whose groundbreaking achievements are remembered for their boldness and the doors they opened for others.

4. Social Change & Activism

Women who led or inspired movements for social justice, equality, or rights, leaving a legacy of positive societal change. Rosa Parks and Malala Yousafzai are figures whose efforts in civil rights and education activism still inspire action today.

5. Mythology and Legend

Sometimes, women are remembered more for the myth or legend that has grown around them than their actual historical deeds. Figures like Helen of Troy or Boudica may have semi-mythological elements to their stories, but their enduring legacy comes from how they are remembered and symbolised over centuries.

6. Global Recognition

The woman's name and legacy transcend national boundaries and time, remaining recognisable across different cultures and generations. For example, Mother Teresa is globally recognised for her humanitarian work, inspiring new generations of charitable workers.

7. Educational and Inspirational Legacy

Some women are remembered for inspiring future generations. They may have laid down frameworks in philosophy, education, or public speaking that continue to be referenced and followed. Simone de Beauvoir, for instance, influenced feminist thought and education for decades after her death.

NOTE 3: ABOUT THE AUTHOR

Andrew Leigh trained as an economist at LSE and wrote a careers column, You & Your Job, for the Observer newspaper for several years. He has an MA in People Management and is a Fellow of the Chartered Institute of Personnel and Development. He worked as a senior manager in the public sector for two decades and established the Adult Services Division of the London Borough of Croydon.

In the late 1980s, Andrew and his business partner launched Maynard Leigh Associates, now a leading UK training and development company (www.maynardleigh.com).

Andrew has authored numerous business books, including Charisma, Ethical Leadership and Taking the Lead.
See: https://tinyurl.com/e6zb285k

His weekly podcast, 50 Ways to Succeed at Work, is available on all the leading podcast platforms and is now in its third year

NOTE 4: ACKNOWLEDGEMENTS

Two noteworthy people have made this book possible, including the 20-named remarkable women.

Thank you to Gillian, my wife, who has helped bring many of these conversations to life with thoughtful and invaluable suggestions, plus diligently checking the material. Without your loving support, this book would never have been written.

Thanks also to Tessa Blanshard-Phibbs, a talented and utterly reliable designer who created and oversaw the book through to production.

NOTE 5: DISCLAIMER

This book is a work of fiction and creative exploration. While inspired by extensive research into biographical, mythological, philosophical, and artistic traditions, the dialogues, events, and characters here are purely the product of the author's imagination. At no time does the author claim to have met the 20 Muses in real life.

While drawing on factual sources, the author does not claim nor intend to imply any real-life correspondence or factual accuracy regarding the historical figures or events.

The content is presented for entertainment and intellectual reflection only. It is not intended as a factual account, scholarly treatise, or a source of historical or biographical truth.

Readers should understand that this work represents a personal and fictional interpretation of abstract ideas, myths, and concepts.

The author expressly disclaims any liability for interpretations, uses, or misuses of the material presented in this book.

NOTE 6: OTHER TITLES BY ANDREW LEIGH

Red Roof Publications
Red Roof, Church Path,
London SW19 3HL

Contact: remarkable@btinternet.com
Website: andrewsbooks.site

For every copy of this book sold,
50p will be donated to the charity: